MISSHAPEN

Nunatak is an Inuktitut word meaning "lonely peak," a rock or mountain rising above ice. During Quaternary glaciation in North America these peaks stood above the ice sheet and so became refuges for plant and animal life. Magnificent nunataks, their bases scoured by glaciers, can be seen along the Highwood Pass in the Alberta Rocky Mountains and on Ellesmere Island.

Nunataks are especially selected works of outstanding fiction by new western writers. The editors of Nunataks for NeWest Press are Aritha van Herk and Rudy Wiebe.

MISSHAPEN
Robert Budde

NeWest Press
Edmonton

© Copyright Robert Budde 1997

First Edition

All rights reserved. The use of any part of this publication reproduced, transmitted in any form or by any means, electronic, mechanical, recording or otherwise, or stored in a retrieval system, without the prior consent of the publisher is an infringement of the copyright law. In the case of photocopying or other reprographic copying of the material, a licence must be obtained from the Canadian Reprography Collective before proceeding.

Canadian Cataloguing in Publication Data

Budde, Robert, 1966–
Misshapen

(Nunatak new fiction series ; 8)
ISBN 1-896300-22-7

I. Title. II. Series.
PS8553.U446M57 1997   C813'.54   C97-910589-7
PR9199.3.B764M57 1997

Editor for the Press: Rudy Wiebe
Cover and book design: Brian Huffman

NeWest Press gratefully acknowledges the financial assistance of The Canada Council and The Alberta Foundation for the Arts, a beneficiary of the Lottery Fund of the Government of Alberta.

Printed and bound in Canada

Author photo courtesy Doreen Holod

NeWest Publishers Limited
#201, 8540-109 Street
Edmonton, Alberta T6G 1E6

I am usable . . . I have been made to speak. I have been sentenced to reality.

—Kaspar "The Wild Boy"

Acknowledgements

This novel was researched primarily at the Circus World Museum in Baraboo, Wisconsin. I have attempted to portray the turn-of-the-century "freakshow" as faithfully as possible, including using much of the language from that particular time period. I have described dates and locations for the circus and dime museums which, if not exact, are at least very plausible. However, this is a work of fiction. The characters are only loosely based on *historical figures* (Jojo, Annie Jones, Prince Randian, and Eisenmann) or loosely borrow from the lives of *real* performers (King Sirrah is based on "Zip" or "What is it?" and Earle is based on James Earle). These representations are fictional and do not attempt historical or biographical accuracy.

Sometimes I think the author plays a much smaller role in the writing of a work such as this than we would like to believe. Much like the circus, many people and resources contributed to it production.

Thanks to Meîra Cook for her generous reading and many mmmmmm's.

Thanks to Menzi Behrnd-Klodt and the Circus World Museum Archives.

Endless thanks to Aritha van Herk, first for taking a chance on me, and then for leaning into the words. Her irrepressible energy and tirelessness gave me no choice but to produce a book. Thanks also to the support of the English Department at the University of Calgary, which is one of the few in the country that has the capability for a Creative Ph.D. in English.

Equally endless thanks to Rudy Wiebe for being the perfect reader and goading me back into the text to rethink and rewrite.

Loving thanks to Debbie Keahey for editing, sleepless nights, and ever.

Never before and never again, my dear good folks. Never before has there been such an exhibition. The most amazing spectacle you will ever lay your eyes on, a wonder you will never forget. Behind this thin canvas awaits the greatest assemblage of oddities ever exhibited, monstrosities that defy words, curiosities of all descriptions. These are creatures beyond belief, a menagerie of human misadventure the scale of which has never been achieved before. Thousands have been awestruck already; in Newark, in Boston, discriminating people everywhere are talking about this very show. Are they human? Are they possible? You be the judge.

Now, you look like discerning people. For you, a special deal. One time only. Just step this way, this way to the freakshow stage, yes, freaks of all kinds, like you've never seen before. Look . . . and prepare to be astounded.

∞
1897
∞

Where the possibility ceases, the impossibility commences.

—Harry Houdini

Projectiles

When slip fell from the sky, no one knew it wasn't divine providence. Caught in the rigging most likely. Must have snuck in when the stakers came, snuck by as they worked in staccato rhythms of six to pound the three foot stakes deep, deep enough to hold up the world. A shadow slipped through them in the drumroll of sledgehammers and the last of dusk. The stitchers made their way slowly, hunched over, lacing the seams with twine, lacing the sky together, the undiscovered bundle nestled within.

The Jacksonville-style canvas must have seemed warm and inviting, its musty breath of a million gasps, its sweet sweat scent, the wet human smell of a thousand sweltering nights when the crowds steamed from fear and that strange, startled joy. But then crack! went the whip and up went the big-top, tired and elegant as eight hungry elephants rising to feed. Swoosh! in a rush slip ascended, up, up, up and the folds shook loose as the cables whined against the bailing rings. The sky opened and out fell slip, a small thud into the stacks and hum of the circus. From one world to another, the descent was elegant and dizzy with possibilities.

The shit and straw cradled the fall so deftly, only Jago noticed and went to investigate.

Only Jago the Magician saw slip fall and he began by telling the story of the flash of light, slip's flesh appearing from thin air—a conjurer's dream! Jago dug at the pile of old oat straw and bulbous fly-covered droppings, dug feverishly to see what providence had invested with him, dug until a porcelain face emerged. A crowd gathered. The cherub baby-face stared back, beaming lily white with a dried bull pie held in two pristine hands like it was some fragile crumbling planet.

Most of the crews were over in the menagerie because when the freaks gathered round there were only a handful of white money workers doing chinese. We were the white money workers; the performers, the ones who got our chance to sparkle on stage or in the rings. But after the crowds filed out, we were bridled and broke a good sweat like the rest of the crew. We complained about doing the gruntwork, being the stars that we were, but it never changed anything.

A few horses were still hoisting the quarterside poles and the stand supports were already hauled in when Jago shouted for us to gather around. He picked up that little rat of a child and slip hung there, hoisted under the armpits, held high like a prize lamb. For all slip knew, the world had gone mad but Jago just started spieling on how this was a miracle and how he'd reached the pinnacle of his arcane artistry in one fell swoop.

The bull drivers, the Zacchini Projectiles, the Malenda girls, all arranged in an awestruck row, even the superintendent, seemed taken in, but Dixie knew Jago and his blowhard ways. It was Dixie who invented your name, slip, "Why it's just a lil ol' slip of a thing—and slip with a small 's' at that!" as she leaned her bulk over your wide-eyed, shrinking face.

Before Jago could protest, Dixie had slip scooped up and tucked away in her bosom (*at which point, slip, you easily disappeared without any sign, hide nor hair*) and off she went cooing ("chouchouchouchouchou") and yelling for some licorice-candy and goobers. Jago just sputtered and stomped around for a while. He never held a grudge but he held on to his story, the story of how he pulled slip from the sky, invented slip out of thin air.

Already, Jago was anticipating a decline in the magician's power to amaze. He had to take adoration where he could. Run with it. The story held the magic, suspended it over the circus rings, tucked it in the palm of the desperate narrator.

Even now, I think I still prefer Jago's explanation to any other. You might not have been divine, slip, but all magic doesn't have to be divine.

Straight from the wet depths of Baton Rouge, Dixie was a southern lady of the most decent sort and the whole troop loved her like a sister from the very first time she heaved herself into Plug's red wagon and became the World's Fattest Lady. She'd been the bubble and laughter in the show for years. The backyard came alive with sexual intrigue and gossip with her tinkling voice in tow. Especially women like me found ourselves cut off from one another and Dixie brought us together whether we liked it or not. In self defense we came out to her elaborate teas and wine parties— much better to be the gossiper than the gossipee. She became a confidante to all of us but we were a bit nervous about her fussing all over slip like that. Like she was holding a doll or pet poodle, poor slip lost in that frightening (if legendary) bosom. Seems Dixie had an indomitable soft-spot for youngsters—liked to cuddle and snuggle, pouring out in folds all the mothering she had in her. But what she had in good intention, she surely lacked in skill. Rough as a grizzly without knowing it. And taken to rages and forgetfulness. We were nervous that she'd fall or roll the wrong way—it'd be the sweet by and by for slip if that ever happened.

Once all the trapeze and highwire gear had been raised, the sideshow gathered in the dining car to discuss what was to be done. The dining car was where we always met. Wilder the cook would hover around the kitchen window arranging and planning, sipping with his eyes unfocused, bending low over huge pots of steaming soups. Without saying a thing he presided over our meetings, sending wafts of thyme and yeast to guide us. He'd set leftover biscuits and preserves next to our elbows when the argument got too heated or break out a stash of hootch if we were too complacent. We huddled around two of the makeshift plank tables arguing about anything from Washington politics to who was the best spitter.

On that day, the day slip fell from the sky, we argued passionately about how in the world we would avoid destroying this child we'd found.

Eyes

The parents could have marched through the tent-flaps with cops in tow any time then but I had a feeling right from the start that slip wasn't like the ordinary lot lice hanging around the circus set-up. At every stop a gaggle of young ones came and tried to latch on, looking to get away from small town drab, looking for a fantasy to fill those big wide eyes. The old towners stood back, looking in close during the unloading. They'd get a far away look in their eyes, dreamed of the freedom they saw in the chaotic scramble of the circus workers. They dreamed of throwing it all away; family, commitment, taxes, and bosses (not noticing the shouting managers and supers who directed our every move). They watched vigilantly, expecting to see that glimpse of the forbidden, some exotica let loose, the wink of a Circassian beauty or a peek at the half and half's legs. The ultimate blow-off.

It never came.

But slip was different and I wasn't surprised when parents didn't turn up looking stern and startled. I just knew. May not have been divine providence but there was a precipice somewhere in slip's wide-open stare, a stare that seemed to have nothing behind it—no malice, no calculation—just taking you in whole as if you were fresh and new too.

That stare you are giving me now.

Makes me feel like I have to fill that stare up with myself. You took us all in, all our wild shapes and deviances, swallowed us like we were palatable, sweet-tarts and slip's eyes like mouths.

I think that was it, slip made us feel like we were surprising again. A new flavour.

∞
1962
∞

Only the true Freak challenges the conventional boundaries between male and female; sexed and sexless, animal and human, large and small, self and other, and consequently between reality and illusion, experience and fantasy, fact and myth.

—Leslie Fiedler, *Freaks*

As if convinced, as if convinced this will be the last, a tired figure walks up to the front doors of the EconoLux Hotel looking for salvation.

The first door does not open.

The second, covered with decals—American Express, CAA, Eliot's Yellow Trade Taxi, Mastercard, The Times Sold Here, Byron's Security Alarms and Smoke Detectors ("Make it solitude—call it peace")—the second door opens with a sucking rush of air. The visitor carries two overfilled folders and a gunny sack smelling of old leaves, old books, standing water. The baggage is unwieldy and seems to be on the verge of spilling across the floor. One hand slips over the edge of the folders. It is thin with long fingers but dark and rough, nails uncut but unpainted. On the back of the unsightly hand is a tattoo reading YOUR NAME IS RICE in large block letters.

The clerk at the front desk does not know whether to address the customer as "sir" or "madam." He clips his sentence off at "how may I help you . . ." His eyes pry for a tip-off but only find mid-length hair, high collar, fair complexion. A dark lavender coat covers what may be a thick skirt brushing the tops of worn black boots. The heavy boots leave wet impressions in the thick burgundy carpet. There are no earrings but many pierced holes and a hint of make-up, cover-up and rouge high on each cheek. Hooded eyes peer from beneath heavy thick eyelashes, waiting for acknowledgement. The clerk is unsettled. He fidgets with a black pen-holder on the counter, plays with the change in his pocket. The cash register hum changes pitch and becomes noticeable. The faint smell of electricity and ink lingers in the air-conditioned air.

No clue. The clerk's unnerved eyes rove over and over the odd figure but come away with nothing, finally come to rest on the tattooed name. He stops after "How may I help you . . . Rice," smiles like a hotel clerk, waits. Waits for the voice.

Rice's voice forms a question, a challenge. This voice is unplaceable—neither male or female, something else, a void tinged only with a fragile sense of being, one that could crumble *at the slightest pressure. And yet, this voice is no comfort to the clerk.*

When Rice replies, "What are you looking at?"—there is no answer, no answer in the entire world that will suffice.

Rice stands in front of the door to the hotel room a long long time before knocking. They have always been frightening; doors, doorframes, tent flaps, these entrances that signal one place is distinct from another.

A young girl runs by and plugs change into a pop machine just down the hall. The light from the machine shines a ghostly blue off her face. She hits a button with conviction after each coin drops, frowns when nothing happens, plugs another. Nothing. Another coin, punch, nothing. Another. Eventually, a can drops into the slot as if from a fantastic height. She clutches the cold can of Coke to her chest as she runs out of sight. The thick carpet seems to swallow the sound of her bare feet.

Along the hallway, the fluorescent lights throb slightly. Rice knows knocking at the door may change everything. This is what Rice wishes: a beginning or ending, it does not really matter which. If this is just another door, if this is just another door . . .

Slow transformation is not an option, not even dreamed of. Time, like a change in air pressure, plummets independent and random outside the skin's slow pulse. This, at least, Rice has already learned.

Rapping twice, the sound is dull as if underwater, a sound that presses against ear-drums. A thin voice, seeming a long distance away, pierces through layers of exhaustion, pricks a nerve of hope. Rice is dizzy, a dizzy traveller come home. Or a vagabond gone beyond hope, trading the world in for the safety of delirium. The door opens to either.

Once inside, the light changes to diffuse sun and from a wide field of bedspread a woman speaks as if she knows Rice, her voice strung with overtones of affection and pity. She is old, old beyond ugliness, old to the point of a wonderful impossibility.

Her ancient skin is creased past mere wrinkles into a landscape of whorls and glowing pear-shaped blemishes. She is pale, almost translucent. Her ears are ragged, honeycombed with earring holes, but without any earrings, like the pierced skin was more adornment than jewelry. The dips and knobs on her skull draw Rice's gaze. And yet her lips are astonishingly full, pristine and moist. Her lips, then, hold Rice's gaze. She speaks again.

"So slip, you let the small 's' spill out and filled the sound up with a proper capital. Rice is your name now, eh? Yes, I think you have grown out of your little name. I won't let it slip, your old name is secret with me. If I call you 'slip' still you'll have to forgive me, old secret names are the hardest to shake."

She talks with an ease that assures Rice she is indeed the Ghost Lady. Her words smell authentic, a sense Rice developed long ago when facts could no longer support truth, when the rules of the search became clear.

Someone else is in the room now.

Coming from the bathroom, a young man ducks and whispers a small apology. The Ghost Lady pats his thigh and asks him what time is it. 9:45. He adds that she shouldn't forget she has another visitor coming at suppertime. She nods and shoos him out. The motion of her arms sends her feathery hair loose from her even whiter scalp. She chuckles. Veins slide and bob in rhythm over her skull, neck, and forearms, forming a living landscape of slow molten life. Rice wonders if that skin would open up, fold around the past like a beating heart, hold it there, still pulsing.

Rice watches now from the other side of the bed beneath a bulbous television clamped to the wall. A knob is missing but, despite its disrepair, the tv seems to glower, threatening to crush both of them. The set is on but the volume off. Flickering on the screen is a family sitting around a dining room table eating a large golden-brown bird. Juices trickle from the crispy skin. So far, there has been no sign of what the ad is for. The vertical hold is just off, so every thirty seconds or so the picture creeps up and re-emerges from the bottom. The grey tv light harshly reflects off Rice's lank black hair and thin face. You would never think such a weathered frame could have grown from the chubby child that the Ghost Lady begins to describe. Rice sits writing down every word.

"And Ricky, think you could sneak us some leftover toast or some of them good eggs from breakfast?" The young man's face turns and winks, then disappears out the half-open door.

Rice hasn't said anything yet, but somewhere deep inside, the word "Becca" mouths itself in a small frightened voice. "Becca" back from muscle and tendon. "Becca" from the marks on skin and bone. Rice tries to hold the word still, still so it will last and last. Rebecca. Becca.

And so Rice is suspended there, bowing in supplication to a tiny old mulatto woman with skin so white it nearly ceases to exist. And both their bodies seem hardly to exist in the room. Only words can hope to fill these spaces.

She speaks again, tending to the tender place opened by the name.

"Becca. Yes, yes, I'm Becca. Don't be afraid, little one. You won't float away. Yes, they told you right, I am Rebecca the Ghost Lady, always be the Ghost Lady, no matter if I am working or not. Come closer, come now, let the Ghost Lady of old, catch you and stake you down in one spot. Poor slip, like a balloon bouncing the top of the tent. But you're back now, back with the show, even though I'm the last of them. You just need some good storying, get you inside yourself. Back from that bit of a kid that was racing your own feet. Like I'd be selling you to yourself. Spieling in front of the bannerline again . . . oh, but selling isn't what you need now. I know what you need. I will remember for you, simple as that. Remember as best I can what a little kid was doing smack dab in the middle of the busiest, most successful freakshow ever. Come now, come closer. There you were, some summer around '97, and Dixie had you tucked away in a flash . . ."

Rice prays that Becca will keep talking forever.

∞
1897
∞

**I fell burning into the desert . . .
Who are you?
I don't know. You keep asking me.**

—Michael Ondaatje, *The English Patient*

Looking Back

The whole sideshow huddled around Dixie holding slip like a stray kitten. The dining car creaked with the weight as our stew and flour biscuits got cold on the wood-plank tables. A half-moon of ghastly, gawking faces hunched over, peering at Dixie's prize.

Oh, how quickly things get turned around and we became the gawking crowd. Odd how unthinkingly we jump the velvet rope.

There, perched out on the fertile plain, the vast midwest of Dixie's belly, slip was gulping down sugar-coated cherry pals and leftover pigeon pie, staring at that ragtag troop. One after another, slip took in the person's odd shape, distorted features, or their strange dimensions. One after another of us felt the wonder of that unassuming gaze.

Towering behind Dixie, Earle jabbered away to get the child's attention. Sometimes we all wished that myth about silent giants were true, but it wasn't. Earle wanted to be a racetrack caller and always talked a mile a minute, fast as that big beefy jaw would go. Got this average-sized voice, figures he would be a normal if he could just get behind a megaphone. His frustration often turned to anger. He almost killed JoJo one night, drunk on gallons of Dakota hootch the sidehands had scored the other side of Sioux Falls. Went berserk when he found himself in the middle of a wide field of nothing. Berserk because of the space. Because of distance pulling him outward. Size and space got away with him, stole his boundaries. He was between worlds, Earle was. The unreal freakshow stage couldn't quite contain him and he never felt as big as his myth. He would stretch his tree-limb arms to grab a stage persona but then his voice came, his voice would betray him. To get back, to get grounded, Earle would test the solidity of the world around him with his fists.

Jojo was hanging near the back by the coffee buckets, afraid to scare the tyke, but interested, leaning and smiling his practiced canine grin. I first met Jojo (Fedor I think he was before) in an old New York dime museum when he was still a young pup just off the boats. Didn't have his act together back then but those red-golden locks! They did the trick on their own. The towners all wanted to pet him and see if he would fetch. Thomas Camden, the museum manager, had a contract on his soul and poor Jojo was mighty miserable. Mrs. Doris' World Museum it was—shut down before the Bowery really hit it big with all that uptown traffic.

Thank god for that. Jojo was let out of the contract and free to find his own fortune. And one of the things his fortune held was meeting me—we stood in line together when they were giving auditions at the new American Museum on Broadway. Next in line ahead of us was King Sirrah. After that, Jojo and King Sirrah did the east coast circuit for a few years while I came out here looking for new openings, maybe even a generous soul or two.

Those two were my dearest friends and I thanked the gods when they joined the midwest circuit with me. They especially came to have a liking for you, slip. Jojo stayed up late talking quietly, hushed and gentle to you over some of that sweet Iowa elderberry cider. He talked so wild and unconnected I lost his meaning, but Jojo was a brilliant man, slip, brilliant in ways that made my head spin, makes you feel yourself slide free into a new skin. I think you learned a lot from him those long August nights.

Howl

Jojo would look into the middle distance when he spoke, as if reading a street sign on the outskirts of town. He'd lean over a steaming cup and stare out, his eyes glittering through his shaggy coat. His voice was shimmering and clear and we sometimes wondered why he wouldn't sing. For hours and hours slip would listen as Jojo told him about the world, as Jojo's voice swirled around and around in currents of thick liquid:

"Late, late, late and slip I have to tell you, I have to tell you about August. August pushes pushes for excess, lush, gold on gold and green, and that smell of almost rank, almost ferment, almost but just this side of regal, ostentatious. Do you believe in evil, slip? I almost choked on a sequin once, a sequin from a horse girl's tights, the manager made me bite her, made me chase after and bite her. In August the berries fall, fall and blend in with the dirt, bugs, beetles and centipedes crawl up, suck all the juice up. Birds eating dirt. And smack our lips at the jam Wilder slathers on those biscuits. And hot; took me a long time to learn not to trim my coat in the summer, cooler with it long and full, then it's fleas I have to worry about. All these things we relearn to be human. The emperor Augustus would make a small sign with his left hand to signal when, which, and how many lions would be released. Just a slight movement, obscured by his heaped robes. The gates would split open, spilling lions into the ring. And gold, rich gold, flowed over the slaves. One after another. We all shrink in the amphitheater, awaiting a sign. The slaves tremble, waiting. The audience waiting to be invented. Waits the slight motion that means we believe in death. Augustas, august us. *Morituri te salutant, Morituri te salutant*! And who do you suppose presides over the freakshow, gives that little flick to signal the type of show he so desires? Mmmmm slip . . . go ahead, stare if you'd like. You are curious, I am a curiosity. I have no tail so don't even ask. Hypersticosis it's called, rampant hair follicles, and it doesn't even give me license to animality. Ask me about August, slip. Ask me about almost."

Conspiracy

Now, let's see, who else was there that day.

Thsk the midget was most certainly there, pensive and polite as ever. Probably didn't join the fuss but watched and kept eating in that elegant way he had invented. A pint size shot of thick English brandy, that Thsk. Reginald was his name overseas but here, in mudville shithole county midwest nowhere, it was Thsk. He seemed trapped in an old dusty romance novel, his handkerchief held over his nose. For such a small man, though, Thsk carried around a giant's share of sadness. His movements were slow violins, his glances half mast.

Course King Sirrah was there. Already mentioned him. The King was made of a few scattered words he broke over the edge of his crooked smile. Look right into your soul though. Hard life but he endured with a chuckle, a flourish of his infernal fiddle, a bob of his flat beloved pinhead, and a toss of his sunken chin.

The Ghost Lady looked up and saw Rice's bewildered look. "Oh, for pity's sake slip, I'd better be giving you stage names if you're following a paper trail."

Let see . . . you might want to write these down . . . Thsk was Captain Pitts until Plug changed it to Sergeant Thimble on account of he thought he noticed more housewives coming in to see the sideshow. Who knows. Jojo's first name was Fedor Jeftichew and he sometimes talked about his childhood in Russia. In your time, Jojo was Jojo the Dog-Faced Boy except when he was starting out and then I think he was the Irishman Setter. Earle James Gideon was the Jacksonville Giant, the Sarisota Cyclops when they made him up in the dime museum, and then later on he was the Goliath of Fort Worth with a bank guard suit and fake bars of gold. He left the show shortly after that. Dixie DeHavilland was a snappier Dixie Lane on stage. With the travelling Barnum & Bailey one summer, when it was still just 32 cars or so, she was Tina Topsy. She died while you and I were on the road the second last summer. Heart attack we figure although they'd hauled her off before we could say so for sure. Or say goodbye.

Now King Sirrah just plain called himself that one day. He had many stage names. Zip and What Is It? were the biggies, the names Barnum had given him. Worked as a glomming geek at the Virginia fairs biting off chicken heads left and right but hit the big time as Barnum's nondescript, the missing link. Played the 1893 Midway Plaissance in Chicago as an African cannibal a few years before you showed. No one knew how old he was, didn't seem to age. Many versions and copies of him popped up quick but he was always the King to us. Barnum invented him but he was ours. It was a while before me and him realized we were from the self-same county in Alabama and, it turned out, shared the same Mama, just at different times. Neither of us were sure if Ma Belsey was our real mum but we both remember her cursing and swatting at the hundreds of kids that swarmed her legs. Both of us remembered a greased picture of Ma standing at the door with more kids than floorplanks to set them on, without a man in sight, and the sky about to spit a hurricane at our thin walls. She shortened my name to Becca when I was two because she hadn't enough breath for the extra.

King was my brother more because of the place, that fly-infested hole of a town, than anything else. And here we were floating around the country, black ghosts with no way home, even if we wanted to go back. Me and King kept our kinship secret—no need to let that little bit of intimate loose in such a thieving place. King's real name was William Henry Johnson, but I'm thinking I am the only one in the whole world who would know that. Enough to make it matter anyway.

Half the show was made up of names. Not many of them we kept for ourselves. They changed so often we had to grab on to one and insist. Many times I remember being addressed and not knowing it, suddenly realizing, oh ya, that's what I'm called now. Oh, ya. That's when I used to cling to my sanity like a vice. Not recognizing your own name? Where was I?

Sometimes the name behind the names, the one I held close like a crumbling hunk of soil, that one true name would dissolve from beneath my feet. When I clicked my heels nothing would happen. Rebecca? Rebecca? Where was I?

And sometimes there was a name behind even that name. One that I don't know. One I need someone else to speak.

Say my name, slip.

Three of the freaks you ended up knowing weren't there the day you dropped in on us. Win Pajaro was Michelangelo the Flying Man come from the People's Museum in New Orleans and travelled with us a few summers. Chris Christina was a half-and-half who caused a ruckus as our blow-off for a while. Chris was our anger I think, made up for all our lazy passive acceptance by piling up a whole heap of spite. Chris told us that if we must, then she was a 'she'. She said this with a contempt for words I had never heard before. She turned abruptly from conversations, disappeared from a conversation just like that. Words hovered around her head like bees, sharp, unnerving, so that she swatted them and the rest of us away.

But it was our bearded lady, Annie Jones, who we all looked up to and who, in a certain way, was our champion. I have a theory that she was the beginning of the end of the freakshow, and, for better or worse, we have her to thank. Annie had a grace about her that is hard to explain. She had a sense of herself that others among us didn't, a confidence as she went around arranging things, her words never furtive or guarded. It was as if she knew about the lie we were all living, knew the absurdity of all, and that she was just playing the game. That made the rest of us nervous because many of us did not know what was going on and seemed to be swept along in the day-to-day without foresight.

She was off having another scrap with Plug that day, I'd imagine—standing toe-to-toe with him, her whiskers bristling with indignation. She was the one who really managed the show but Plug sometimes felt threatened and tried to get in her way. Then the fireworks started. Plug's real name was Clyde Ingalls but we always called him Plug because of his nose and that hollow wet voice of his.

But names are just names in the end. You have all those on the posters and schedules. We are going to have to get deeper than that to dig up the real showlife you lived.

Oh, and me, I guess I should formally introduce myself. Rebecca Bernard Johnson, the Ghost Lady, the Albino Pin-Cushion, at your service, slip.

Resistance

Wilder the cook leaned out of the kitchen and yelled for everyone to clear out so he could get the tables out to the candy butchers. We ignored him. Living space turned into a commodity in our business and you stood your ground or you'd be shuffled right off the grounds. And not just physical space either, noise space. You'd be rendered a mute in no time if you didn't shout out a niche. In the travelling shows, the ground beneath your feet and the rush of air in your throat was all you had.

We kept right on jawing, mostly arranging for babysitting around our schedules and figuring how to rework an act so Plug wouldn't have a choice but to let slip stay. Knew we couldn't work slip into Thsk's headlining act because children and midgets don't mix—the perspective looks awry and the audience gets antsy. A ten-in-one at the state fair down in Kansas City tried it once and it flopped. Most promising thing we came up with had slip standing in one of Earle's hands. Slip was perfect for making the giant seem bigger and that was what Plug looked for—anything to make an act bigger, undeniably amazing, authoritatively the ONLY, indisputably the MOST!

So slip first performed with Earle the very next night. What a natural on stage! Glowing and smiling and everybody gawking and fearing Earle'd fall. Earle wasn't that good a performer and barely came off as more than an awkward tall man when the crowd was fully expecting a giant or a goliath. Earle didn't have the knack of projection. His heart wasn't in it. But slip made up for him, framed him into myth—tiny hands barely visible as they clutched Earle's huge upturned thumbs. Everyone fell in love.

Recollection

So that's the story of how you came to us sideshows. From the instant Dixie spoke your name into existence we always meant best for you slip, no matter what, in all those crazy times, hard times, times that swooped down to crush us, swallow us up into that big mouth of a crowd, we always always looked out for you. More than once we had a hell of time scuffing it and I wondered if it was the right thing for you travelling with us, seeing all that shit and nastiness, not getting a proper education and all. The way you studied the performances, read the pamphlets and posters like they was scripture, the way you made the show your own, the way you looked up the bigtop center-pole lit up with the pan lamps like it was something real to hold on to, tight like a precious thing, all this made me believe you was with it, with the show through and through. If a place filled with lies and fakery could be called home, the show became yours. If you were a towner before, you left that slip behind in the pile of crap we pulled you from.

Repetition

Lots of conjecture on your home—where you were from, why your mama left you, or how she lost you. Days passed before you finally spoke. We'd all assumed you was mute until the King goofed you into a laugh that tumbled into a stream of ringing talk with so many demands it left us gaping.

A bunch of the sideshows went out in daylight on a layover in Meadville. Back then, the midwest was still unsure of itself, and all the small-town folk felt like strangers in their own country. In the east coast cities we'd never dare go out. If we did, inevitably someone would start in on us, taunting and poking. We'd retreat but they would pursue, throwing stuff. People on the coast felt compelled to protect a certain way of life. They seemed to think they had enough trouble with all the immigrants passing through and cluttering the streets without having to face a troupe of freaks taking up the sidewalk.

Out in the midwest or on the lakes we'd have a couple of the beefier bull-hands come along just in case of trouble but we weren't expecting any. Anyway, there was this statue of Oliver Perry from the War of 1812 set up in a small park along Main Street. King Sirrah galloped right up to it and leapt into its folded arms. What a sight!—his gangly brown limbs sprawling in comic aplomb, his gaping grin even larger with the absence of a forehead, the knot of hair at the point of his head bobbing in the breeze. He smiled as if for a portrait and then turned with a flourish to plant a big kiss on the cheek of the glowering stone visage.

We were used to the King's antics but slip's voice burst the floodgate, howling with delight, "Do it again!" The strain in slip's voice slapped the air like a guy stake in granite, a voice that made you move to help, arms spread wide, even before the words sunk in. "Do it again," became a litany. Always slip running up and pleading "do it again" without reference, leaving everyone with no clue. Back stage, in the middle of a conversation, while we slept, anywhere we were, slip arrived, abruptly demanded, "Do it again." And we tried. Showing off our latest trick or pose. Retelling a joke or story. Recreating the expression we'd just made, our faces scrunching up to please the child. Easing the edge of panic in the plea.

We asked about your home, slip; your parents, your school, but you didn't seem to know anything about them, or didn't want to tell us, or had blocked it up. You'd search for a while, trying to think of answers but came up with nothing. Didn't upset you, you didn't think it was strange, and quickly turned to me or Jojo or the King. A big jump into our arms. "Do it again."

We figured your accent for Canadian, guessing that you were from across the border into Welland or St. Catharines. You piped up hoity-toity words like 'chesterfield' and lilting sentences that arched into incredulous and haughty tones. The type of sentences that either rolled into a demand or curled into an earpiercing question. I don't remember if we went back east through Canada that year or not. Must not have or I would have remembered the fear of losing you to a strange couple or a teary-eyed mother. No, we musta swung south that year, tried to pick up Austin and Kansas City from the B & B.

No time to worry about a sorry looking seven year old with the business so competitive and Barnum looking to sink us. But I always felt compelled to remind you of where you was from. Called you "my little beaver" in my best mock-British accent. I couldn't let all sense of origins slide away—everybody needs a dose of home to survive. Or so I thought. I don't think it helped. Anywhere you were at the time became home. The show became a picture book, and you lived each page one turn at a time.

Trunk

King Sirrah didn't often finish his sentences.

"There's wisdom in the least."

He'd find a gap in the babble, a lull, and announce his intentions to speak with a quick burst from his violin.

"The time it takes between now and."

We'd listen and privately fill in the remainder of the sentence with whatever we thought appropriate.

"More numbers lie underneath every."

"A price and a judge over."

Then discussion would resume, unflustered, but with King's sentence hinged on our mind.

"Just wait for the snug, turn with."

Sometimes just a word blurted out: "foreign" or "cataclysm." Sometimes a phrase, a pronouncement of the highest importance: "For the love of freaks!" More often than not, to our surprise and delight or dismay (depending on who), the words were swearwords: "Shit, crap, and how-do."

"Press fuck the press right in."

His voice was slow, thick-tongued, and nasal, seemingly dopey, but it could also capture a resonance, a deep authoritative clout.

"Just when you think!"

Most of the time the King stood to the side, head tilted as if listening to a background noise, or an attempt to look endearing, like one would in front of a baby. He let go little squeaks from his violin.

Zzzzzsspppsk-sk-skr-Skkkkkrrrrrong. "When there must be time for."

"Seethe a kid in." Zzzsk.

All he owned was that violin and a beat-up old trunk full of ripped letters and scraps of paper. In the middle of set-up, you could usually find King sitting on his trunk, activity careening around him, his head at a jaunty angle and a goofy grin galloping across his face.

"Pandemonium, pandering to the story's first. Guffaw." Zzzskskrng.

Dispersion

Wilder lost two of his fingers in the spokes of a camel wagon that had jumped its brake shoe. Ripped off, not cut. Lost in the mud.

Wilder lost two more of his fingers to a gorilla's teeth and leaned over to love his thumbs. Would cradle his thumb in the other hand, or in other people's hands, or in the warm nest of his armpit.

Wilder lost two more of his fingers on the tracks, crushed into nothing and we ribbed him, called him half-hand, stump, asked him to count past three, gave him the 'ok' sign all the time.

Wilder lost two more fingers to an errant cleaver and learned to hook pots and ladles deftly with less leverage, balance he always said, a matter of balance, as he twirled a spatula around his pinky and timed the broth and omelette perfectly.

Wilder lost two more to his pistol, dirt in the barrel splitting metal open up to his wrist. He gave up hunting and loved simple designs, common figures of speech, the beauty of one colour next to another. He learned how the mind plays tricks on the body, or visa versa, and tries bravely to hold on to the ideal shape, those five lovely fingers. He learned scar tissue is softer to the touch than normal skin.

Wilder lost two more of his fingers, wouldn't tell us how, and made startling shapes by lamp-light, two-headed dragons and the London Bridge.

Two fingers lost Wilder and turned into worm food. There is no accounting for perfection.

Consequence

One night we borrowed Annie's scrapbook of the circus and sat on my bunk looking through it late into the rolling night as the train scraped toward Des Moines. My quilt fit nice around us and the book lay open between us. I turned pages, but you seemed dissatisfied, restless as I lifted pictures close to see expressions, traced faces with my fingers against the slick surfaces.

I miss those nights we wondered aloud at the crazy mess we were in. The two of us, the Canadian Cherub and the Ghost Lady, stuck in this travelling insanity, cut off from the world and yet seeing sides of these small shit towns never seen before. The pictures held them in grainy sweeps of black and white but you refused, demanded more.

"Becca?"

"Mmmmm"

"I was just wondering . . ."

Always wondering, you were. Hardly knew what about before you were on to the next. And so late at night. I couldn't stand any more questions.

I cut you off. "Are you worrying about something specific that you'd wonder and ask so many questions?"

"No, nothing I know. But . . . Becca it's like everybody has it easier. Easier I mean to keep things all together. Jojo told me today about his parents and the boat to America and all the people vomiting into the bay. How come I can't put together a story like that? All those people and things and places and names and stories and I just want to keep them all in my head. How do you do it, how do you keep it all together Becca?"

"Well, I just put things next to each other and tie them together with my self, wrap a thought around them or leave my scent on them or arrange them the way I like on the window sill. And through it all I filter out the precious things or the strong things that hold me up. Pull them out and pile them inside, in that big warm place with the wide open shutters and all the drawers and cupboards you could ask for." I held up a picture from the scrapbook. "I just remember things that fit into the picture."

"What do you mean by remembering, Becca?"

What. What do you mean. Remembering. Remembering?

There comes a time when all things inconceivable come to rest lightly, ever so lightly, in the hands of the misbegotten. Becca's hand's fell to her sides and the book flopped closed in her lap.

"Oh, dear child . . . oh, I am so sorry, that's it isn't it. Oh, how ever are we gonna keep you from flying apart? No memory! You have no memory. Come closer love, there there, come close and we'll figure something out. How could I have been so blind?"

Recollection

There are all kinds of memory. It's one of those things we assume is true and everywhere. Everybody's is just like our own and we can't imagine any other. But there's all kinds: just takes a deep talking to, close over hot rum or under warm rain, so close you almost touch, it takes words to find out how memory is a jumbled bag of time. There's a sneaky slide-up-behind-you-kind of memory, there's a stomping-in-the-bones memory that sets your hips a swaying, there's thin threads of memory whispering in your ear like a preaching gnat, there's a boxed-up-and-knocking-to-get-out memory. There's memory that's a fine needle point no one's supposed to touch but slips under your skin and makes people look away. There's memory that's piled up and thick so as it seems to be right there in front of you even though it's as made up as can be. Memory that cuts in and out like a stitch. Memory that floats and teeters high above the rings. Memory that drops and flops into your lap like a gift from the sky just opened up. Sometimes it's in colours like flags and spangles, sometimes it's touches and fabrics, wafts and breezes, sometimes it's a deep where you can't reach.

And sometimes it's in words. Plain words convincing you of yourself again. Or tricking you, it doesn't really matter.

It seems slip had no memory. Two days tops, two days to hold on to before it slipped away, two days to invent a life like weaving a cloth that is unravelling as fast as it's created. A swatch of cloth two days long. The sideshow fed slip back the cloth, wore slip's living like an insignia, like a uniform, vestments to remind us all how tenuous our lives really were. All of us, grasping for the wind that swept by slip faster than breath.

And so here you are now, floating without a clue what's behind or ahead. In the show, we were good at telling stories. So that's what we did—we told you stories. Over and over we told all about the show, the freaks, anything we could think of. Filled you up with stories. True stories, terrifying stories, magic stories, outright lying stories, stories about what we believed. You took them and built a raft. You took shelter, like a second skin, and that's all we could do. And that's all I can do now. I am just afraid you won't fit into the skin I knit for you.

Recognition

The sleeping car never stopped moving. Swayed to a bullying west wind or the rocking motion of late night wandering or sex. Twenty bodies per with all their sweat and breathing and coughing and mumbling and arguing and snoring. The cubicles were six feet by twelve feet with a bed, three drawers, a wall lamp, and a foot square window with a pull-down blind. The train tugged us along, grumpy from the last stop, but irritable to get to the next. Schenectady, Chilliclothe, Beloit—the weatherworn signs rolling up stationside, the odd waiting figure or peering face. Kids pointing.

Late at night, lying in bed, the engines pounding GOGOGOGOGOGOGOGOGOGOGOG, the steel on steel, a sound like so many children squealing YYYYYYYYYYYYYYYYYY-EEEEEEEEEEEEEEEEEEE. And the steam rushed every so often: sssssssssssssssss. But then every few miles, the whistle blew as the train passed a crossing or a bridge: NOOOO-NOOOOOOOOOOOOOOOOOOOO . . . . NOOOO-NOOOOOOOOOOOOOO. Star or moonlight flashed and bobbed through the window, looming shadows blocking the light into garish shadows or a tunnel. A black rumble hurling blind through sleep and wide-eyed sleeplessness.

Slip lay stalk stiff with flashes of imagined landscape shifting and swirling above in the dark. The cabin smelled of slip and the pungent scent of animal shit; elephant gobs, horse apples, llama pellets, dogshit, the lion's pungent piles, monkey crap. The smell clung to shoes and nostrils. Exuded in sweat.

But the blackness leaked out fear and uncertainty. Late when only the rolling, bucking of the rail motion existed, late when the colours and images jumped and blended in half-sleep, late when sudden murders leapt awake and slip stiffened with the certain knowledge that someone had opened the door and was standing near the foot of the bed. The certain knowledge. Standing right there. A shadow tremor? An eye glint? Don't move, for death lurks everywhere you are not. Denial by absolute stillness. Praying for sleep to bludgeon. Waiting with quick breaths until colours obscure the desperate search for signs of a knife, teeth, an even keen gaze. Moments stretched across the bed like a corpse and reached up through the mattress to knuckle backbones.

And slip watched, trembling, as a single shadow detached (a tree copse outside?) floated forward, slow, drifting, slowly came close, closer, leaned in, farther, farther, as if over an open book, farther, then tipped on to the bed (warm breath?) and, at the last second, merges with slip into sleep.

Morning breaks with a long sigh.

Excavation

I was Jojo's personal barber by default. Out behind the tin clamour of the calliope we got a bucket of soapy water and I washed him up, getting the bigger snarls and knots out before I sharpened the scissors. An audience gathered. All I did was trim, neaten up the scraggly parts, thin out in places. Jojo had trouble keeping his skin healthy so I had to be extra careful not to nick him. He said a nick would take months to heal properly.

I was nervous that first time. Dropped the scissors several times and Jojo ended up with a funny bald spot at the back of his neck that I made everybody promise not to tell him about. But I got used to the funny swirls and waves in his rich red hair. Soon it became a ritual. We moved behind the latrine for privacy, a quiet time with just the sound of the scissors snipping and clipping, the lazy fluff collecting at our feet. He had long sleek strands that fell for miles around his chin and ears. Higher on his face the hair was coarser, a bit darker. Then, around his eyes and mouth, down his neck, it was fine and feathery. These bits would float up in the breeze instead of falling after they were cut. Float up and up, sun dogs chasing the sun, until they were lost in the clear blue.

He'd lean his head back, eyes closed, and let me traipse through his hair, down the sides of his head, neck, shoulders, around his mouth and nose, over his throat. The skin beneath his hair was sore sometimes. When it wasn't it was a tender pink like baby skin. I used a soft brush and made sure there were no snarls before I began by running it through right down to the skin. Sometimes I swore he purred.

Soon the word got around though, and I was in demand. On off-days there would be a line-up to my chair behind the latrine where I stood cutting off pounds and pounds of hair. Made a pretty penny preening and layering, shaving and de-lousing. Then, on top of that, I made fifty cents a pound extra selling the hair I collected to the next Johnson & Beckers Co. outlet we ran into. J & B had stores in Chicago, Detroit, Minneapolis, a converted Smith & Wesson warehouse in Buffalo and were opening new ones farther south. The clerks usually sneered distastfully at the source of the hair. They were careful not to touch it, sure it was unclean in numerous ways. But who were they to quibble? They were buying our hair for god's sake!

There was something gratifying about the work, some void in my life that hair-cutting filled. Maybe it was the quiet conversation, the chit-chat and storying. Maybe it was the bodies; the intimacy of my hands through their hair, my hip against their forearm, the feel of their breath on my gentle probing hands.

One day Angus Payton came around wanting a quick shave. He was meeting a business associate for lunch that day and fell asleep on the overnight from Columbus. He flopped into my chair and ordered, "Close as you can get, honey." Honey! I was glad he was seated looking away and couldn't see my tight lips and white knuckles as I ran the razor blade over the whetstone. Honey, eh.

I had never seen the man up close before. He had soft wrinkles and crowsfeet around his eyes. He was sweating and there were broken blood vessels in the skin on his nose. The blade snicked over his stubble tight and close, blood rushing to the surface of the skin ahead of it. Up his neck, back from his chin, close against his thin slack lips. He grunted at one point and I eased up on the blade. It is amazing how many major blood vessels and tendons are close to the surface at the neck. A whole landscape there, just on the flipside of what we can see. I had never thought about it before.

I caught a glimpse of Jojo and Chris watching from the food car. Jojo wagged his finger at me as if to say, 'don't you dare!'

I leaned over his right shoulder, I blocked out the sun, I filled his sky.

Oh, don't worry about a thing. There, there. "Now hold still while I get your adam's apple."

Payton's eyes snapped open at something in my voice.

But I smiled sweet and nice. "Almost done, hold still."

Honey. Hold still. I'll be a good girl.

Honey. I'll be good.

I will.

Rice watches as Rebecca tugs at a stray thread that's come loose on the quilt she lies under. She worries at it as she talks. The thread is scarlet while the rest of the quilt undulates in shades of peach and off-white. Rebecca tries to pull the strand free of the quilt, refusing to snap it off.

Rice watches her do this, listening to her speak. The fate of the thread becomes important to the story, seems connected. But Rice's eyes stray up the hand, onto the knobbed surface of her hand, the veined surface running up the back of her hand, up her wrist. As she tugs, muscles scurry under the mottled skin and tendons slide out, verging on an escape to meet the everyday air.

The thread, once critical to the story, is now forgotten.

Resistance

It was Chris who asked whether you were a boy or a girl. The question came as we stepped from the dining car into the white blast of sun. Annie had been making one of her speeches about women's rights and the men at the table had turned surly and defensive.

We hadn't even thought to wonder about it. Some of us must have thought girl, some of us boy. I stood stunned, trying to decide which I had thought, if any. To this day I think I hadn't really decided. It hadn't even been a question. Isn't that odd. That face was like whole milk still steaming out of the teat and soft apricot silk all in one. Could be any sex.

Earle up'd and tossed slip over to tug down the kid's trousers. But Chris protested, "No, no, it does't matter—I was just marvelling that I couldn't tell's all. Not wondering. No, leave slip jus' be slip." And Earle dropped slip, startled by Chris' urgency.

Chris looked shaken and left ahead of us.

Chris Christina would probably survive us all; born to cattlefolk in east Montana and tough as old canvas. Chris' parents didn't exist for her any more (disowned probably is the word but Chris would never call it that) but two brothers and two sisters popped up often to spend the night drinking and making trouble. We didn't mind at all because usually these visits would pull Chris out of her latest funk, long stints of depression that dragged through into weeks. She ran the ragged edge back and forth between giddiness and absolute desolation. Like the rest of us, Chris was a mix of scars and glitz, despair and revelry, suicide and ecstasy. And it seemed all to land square on her chest. Chests.

She left the security of the grounds more than any of us, gliding off as soon as the latrines had been dug and the animals bedded down for the night. With a wink to the night watchman, Chris walked off the grounds looking for a drink, looking for a table next to the stage, looking for an elegant soiree to careen around drunk and loud, looking to be the star and the fool all in one. She would run off with the mayor's son or a countess, run out into the rain with everyone watching, in the spotlight and loving it desperately. Queen or king for one night, she would come back the next morning, jilted, shins bruised, make-up smeared, making light of the whole affair. We usually learned more from the morning paper.

Every night, it seemed, she went looking. Looking for a transcendent lover, for a moment of fame, for the perfect party. She alternately scoffed and adored high society. Called the swankiest "swellegant."

Every night, she went looking. Looking for a lover, any lover, looking for an unflinching lover.

Chris' anger was one of the few things that slip did not ask to see again. It was enough the first time; a vicious curse, wiry flailing arms and teeth, spit. And yet, there was that thin connection between them; one both, the other neither.

I was the only one who bathed you so of course I knew, knew the tender spot between your legs, the sleek measure of your hips and chest. In behind the hippo carriage we'd fill a metal tub with lukewarm water (going cold) and lathered you up until you sparkled. It is hard not to think of you as pristine, hard not to envy your unblemished form, the quiet secret of sex you held to yourself. But all the while you were with us no one else knew.

"You and I were both ghosts of sorts. A ghost of sex and a ghost of skin. These things that set us apart or set us free." The Ghost Lady reaches out and places her twig fingers over Rice's hand. They have no weight. She leans back and dust plumes from the bedding.

"Or maybe I was being naive."

Economics

You were growing up faster than we could follow, and posed some peculiar problems for us unpracticed parents. The sideshow troop took shifts caring for you so you weren't ever left alone. Jago came and saw you almost every day. Wasn't often the bigtop performers came across to mix with us sideshowers but Jago couldn't keep away. He'd come by like a new father all jaunty and sparkling, his thin moustache twitching with pride. He decided you ought to learn a trade and began teaching you the fine art of relieving a fool of extra possessions. I gave Jago a warning lecture about bailing you out if things got sticky but I agreed, hoping it would teach you how to get along on your own. Plus I figured you'd be damn good at thieving. Slip in and out in a blink of an eye.

Jago spent long nights teaching slip the approach, the draw, the take, the leave. The dance steps. "The invention of something out of nothing," Jago would lecture. They'd approach each other over and over, make the contact over and over. At first Jago made it easy, leaving himself open, holding his arms wide, using loose pockets. But gradually he made it harder and harder for slip, closing his arms and putting the goods deeper and deeper. Taught how to talk the lift; pardons and queries to put the mark off. Long into the night Jago danced with his creation, pretending they were strangers, eyes averted, silent, and then the quick flurry of closeness, fabric, hands and away, the retreat, slip grinning. A kind of transcendence, Jago teaching another conjuring, a conjuring that filtered through private places and plucked out something precious that wasn't even missed. A kind of perversion, but just outside the body's desires. An orderly transaction, filled with an infinite trust in wealth.

I am, and have always been, a poor woman. That is how you were educated, slip.

Are there any things that cannot be stolen?
No, don't tell me.

Origins

Here it is: I think slip's memory didn't work because of the freakshow. Forget about genetics, or poetic diseases, or dramatic traumas, or some outlandish magic. The freakshow stole the need for a memory.

I am not a mother; a Ghost Lady like me could never give the comfort that a mother is defined by. I think slip's memory left when comfort was no longer an option. Because it was too hard to be a white normal-shaped kid amongst all us freaks. Because it was easier to just get lost in the rush of chaos. Because slip could not connect what went on around those peering little eyes, because the agony and joy was too much, because there was nothing in common between my porous body and slip's sleek perfect body. And so memory became a useless limb. Sometimes adaptation means amputation. Guilt even.

So slip forgot memory in order to appease. In order to share in the rootlessness of freaks. Another fraud.

The audience only got a taste of the freakshow, a glimpse of a facade, a front, and then they were out. The life slip led was completely immersed in the show. The difference between taking a dip in a pool and growing gills.

After a show, slip would put on my clothes and pose with the black dress drooping onto the floor, the highheel shoes twice too big.

Once, I walked in to find slip looking wide-eyed, in shock, a needle sticking into the thick part of a blood-drained forearm. It was not far in before slip had stopped, blood trickling around the edges, the image of a pin-cushion performer on stage drifting away quickly as the pain surged in.

It was like slip wanted to take on all our roles. As if to contain us. As if that slip of a body wasn't enough anymore.

Perspective

The Talker and the Professor stood between the Ten-in-One line and the crowd like a buffer. Directors and the script. Ten freaks in various poses, the Talker in a top hat and tails, the Professor in a long white coat and spectacles. They spoke as if something had just been discovered, as if this were an inaugural unveiling, as if history were being made.

Practise music drifted in from the band pit in the bigtop. The trumpet carried the best, loud and erratic. And the audience would shuffle and whisper if the talker didn't hold them. Sometimes they would talk back, tell him to get on with it. But mostly the talker had them, blowing the language up to immense proportions, his voice soaring with the enormity of it all. Then, when his spiel was on the verge of too much, he would address the professor, as if in conversation, discussing the authenticity of the acts the audience was about to witness. His voice was monotone and sprinkled with latinate words, some piling together into incomprehensible concoctions of latin, french, and english. It sure sounded learned. Specific names of afflictions, measurements, and, always, locations of discovery were important to the professor's speech. Always, a detached account of the capture in the depths of the Congo basin or the chance meeting in the hermit-filled backwoods of North Carolina punctuated the end of the professor's spiel.

Pan lamps flickered from the side poles and two hung on the center poles. During the day the light filtered in from the roof canvas in a diffuse glow that cast odd shadows and delicate shadings. The performers were mostly backlit. The audience squeezed in to be surrounded on three sides by the row of freaks. A crowd of mostly men shuffled from side to side to see each one or to stop and linger, focusing on a favourite. Four out every five hats were the same brand-name. The velvet ropes bulged and the clasps clanked against the posts. The raised u-shaped stage lifted the performers two feet above the crowd. Cloth draped over the edge of the stage to conceal a handful of stagehands lying underneath in case of trouble. The dust from the ground was easily brushed off shiny leather shoes but it sunk into the laces, stained them for good. Simple props occupied each performer's portion of the stage. Annie had her camera tripod, a boudoir, and a painted country villa scene behind her. Earle had a club, papier mâché boulders, and furs, so he and slip could do their David and Goliath skit. There was no upstaging, for each performed the centerpiece of their act in sequence. The scared ones in the audience hung near the door, didn't want to get caught inside.

It's as if we are back there, slip. Back in the show. Close your eyes.

Glances pass between freaks over the heads of the crowd as cues. Acts or speeches are adjusted depending on the feel of the crowd—whether they fidget, grumble, are completely enraptured, or seem nonplussed. Annie is the best judge of the crowd and she sends quick signals (a thumbs up, a swirl of a finger to speed up) to the rest of us that dictate how long to draw the acts out. The Ten-in-One clicks along swinging on the flashing eyes of Annie, building up to a pitch, at which point the crowd is turned toward the dime blow-off and Chris' private stage behind a curtain on the left side near the front of the tent. The dark curtain beckons as Dexter goads them toward that most renowned of freaks, half man half woman. The ultimate atrocity.

Ah, finally, the crowd seems to sigh. So far it hasn't been the magic they expected but now, now they will see what they have been looking for.

Chris' act is filled with silence. The crowd's expectations slowly collapse in on themselves. Hope for the exotic first glints, fizzles, and then disappears in the cheap tassles she wears. The appearance of this anaemic stark figure and her plain display leaves them stirring, unsettled, yet vaguely comforted. A necessary violence, their eyes gawking out at Chris, seeing but not seeing. Their eyes reaching out to probe, to caress the perfect symmetry of her body. An essential exhibition of natural order gone mad—the ideal male and female attributes in one human body. The Garden of Eden, manicured and sultry, and they were there as witnesses.

It would make a good story at the office the next day.

Afterward, the freaks watch the audience file out, silent but flushed with the buzz of intense anticipation and the still hypnotic words of the Talker. Flushed they return to family or lovers, or walk away in the drizzle, hands in their pockets, touching carefully the place where the dime would have rested.

Resistance

I had a few stock holes all established and healed up nice and tough. Belly, thighs, and biceps. Just like earring holes you know. In '89, I got them done in a Bowery backroom after Plug had told me just being an albino wasn't enough to get me into the show. Getting turned away by Plug that first time really shook me up. I was a black woman with white skin and had nowhere to go.

So I punched myself full of holes! Ha. Now I can laugh.

A strange combination of needing a gimmick and wanting to reduce some baggage. The guy was polite and used a local and lots of disinfectant. It hurt. The one in my belly did not heal for a long time and I battled infection for months, bathed in foul smelling oils. The one under my arm got infected every spring, reminding me that those holes weren't supposed to be there. Twelve holes in all not counting my ears. Twelve extra places for the world to invade.

I had to use them every day or they'd start to close up. So, even on off nights or travel days I had to go through the routine, sitting by myself, vaguely checking for sight-lines and ideal angles, sliding the needles briskly through the outskirts of my body.

They're closed now. I am closed for business, slip. All except this one near my heart. That one I still keep open to remind me of who I used to be.

The rest of my gig was gaffs; turned needles and retractables, illusions like the ones I seemed to pass through my throat. You hooked them with the 'real' holes and then the gaffs are a sure thing. Easy.

I heard Mortado was using hoses on Coney Island to

pump water through his holes like he was leaking but I never could get the hands to rig me something like that. I was content to stick to the basics. It was the combination that caught them; albino AND a pin-cushion. Tickled images of transparent skin, anemones, the possibility of disappearing entirely. Lots of men like their women frail, insubstantial. A ghostly exotic beauty like me was in high demand. I learned quick that I needed my voice to protect me, prevent any old arsehole from sweeping me off to be his pale ideal. Had to learn to growl, spit, turn the trick off with a derisive jeer. Had to learn to pump my lungs shouting coarse and unladylike, make them glance around for onlookers. At the same time, I had to maintain a certain elegance so as not to lead them to thinking I was a witch. No, that would not have been good at all, not at all. And it was hard, hard not to be called a witch. Wore lots of white even though black is my best colour. Didn't wear my outlandish jewelry; my ivory dolphin, my charms, my dyed feathers. Took care and effort not to be a witch. Takes a lot of work to seem like something you're not, on stage, and seem not to be something you are off it.

The men loved what I did. Came to my wagon in droves, waited outside the train car for hours, worried at my health. Late at night I chanted over their prone bodies, casting my own sort of spell that made them disappear as quickly as they came.

My Body

The thing is, people *wanted* to see the gaff. They wanted to discover the trick, to see the wires, to invent the sleight-of-hand. They wanted to see the creases and props in the performance, the ragged edges between my body and me.

Artifice is that comforting.

The Ghost Lady was that comforting. When I performed I wanted one person in the audience, just one, to see the turned needle that slides past the jugular behind my neck. They never said anything, just smiled in that knowing way. Those that see, that really see, were the ones who came shyly to my room after the show. Like a cube from a square, they felt they knew me better with that added dimension of deception. Deceive me again, they seemed to plead. Deceive me, love me, tell me you will never die. A wink from the stage, a break in the actress' countenance, a shadow cast by the camera. They knew you knew and it all became that much more desperately beautiful.

When I tell you this story and suddenly turn and look you full in the eyes . . .

The Carnival

It never was like that—the free spirit of the circus, the folk traditions, the revelry, order turned upside-down, freedom.

Freedom my ass.

There was no such deliverance. No such interlude. It was just another order. The gaze insured an order. Sure there was no monarchy, sure there was no dictator, sure there was no slavery, sure there was no preaching, sure there were no morals, sure there were no class distinctions, sure there was no resistance. But the idea of freedom, free zones of the circus' playful existence . . . well, I've never found them. Maybe only certain people were allowed in.

Instead of monarchy, there was Barnum and his high ideals of showmanship, homage not in ritual but in dollars. And then there were all the Barnum wannabe's following in his footsteps like a long bloodline. Instead of a dictator, there was Payton, manager par excellence, his rule ironclad in the name of efficiency and profit. Instead of slavery there was working for nothing, no trickle down, a low mortality rate. I believe there are many different ways of owning another person. Instead of preaching there was spieling, to the gods of science and story-telling on the altar of the sideshow stage. Instead of morals, there were codes of honour, rules of the game, the proviso that the buck comes above all. Instead of class, there was pecking order, on which a small albino mulatto was amongst the lowest. Instead of resistance, there was the protest of the church authorities, there was mere survival, there was an ounce of joy, there was very little else except complicity.

The strangeness of the order made it seem like no order at all. Oh, how people desired chaos yet clung to the safety of design. Desired enough to make themselves blind.

Someone told me that carnival used to mean ripping flesh from bone. These bones believe it. Except not with knives or teeth but with eyes. Tore me to pieces some nights. But America was finding out that it was just as easy to get shot on the wide-open western frontier as it was to get shot by a thug in New York—the uncontained and unfamiliar just as brutal as the everyday. There were no more pristine places.

When the people came in throngs and asked what it was like to be with the show, to be a carnie, I told them to go home.

Poetics

Only Jojo and Annie were eloquent enough to spiel on their own. Annie had to be careful not to overdo it, but she was smart enough to lower her eyes, play the part. She experimented with different acts and staging more than the rest of us. Performance was in her blood. She knew how to play an audience, read them and tug at their expectations. Her performances never gave them exactly what they wanted, never completely, always a bit off, a bit disconcerting, leading them gently away from their mindset coming into the tent. Jojo called her a mole—"damned subversives, we'll be over-run!"—but he always said it with admiration, smiling at her like a conspirator.

I admired the control they seemed to have. I felt like a character in a story by comparison. As the Ghost Lady, my birth was attributed to the combination of a full solar eclipse at the instant of conception and my mother's habit of chewing the hot tar that workers spread on the streets of Port Au Prince. But the audience had trouble making the connections. Then we went with the "woman with flesh of pure silk" and had ballysticks come up and feel the skin of my arm to confirm that the skin was indeed pure silk. But that story got tired after awhile. It lacked drama. The next season my condition was inflicted by the curse of a bijou witch doctor which turned my blood to air and made me impervious to any blade so that I could not die and would suffer immortality until a virgin soul stabbed me in the side with a silver spear. This version went over well, especially after I started making myself up all undead-like and evil.

Dexter the Talker and that damn Professor filled in the story with all the proper dramatic pauses and drawling sincerity. Dexter would begin after coming in from the bally stage and would set up the basics of each freak. To bolster authenticity he would call on the Professor to provide the scientific explanation for each phenomena.

These bearded gentlemen, one in a three-piece suit, the other in a white lab coat, constructed the plot of our bodies and our lives. The audience's eyes slogged toward us but their ears collected the Talker's words. Eyes glazed, leapt, fired in response to the words. Eyes trained.

A slight pressure there, behind the image, the words taking shape, a slight push, jostle, just behind.

And slip was off with another glittering prize. And slip was a ghost in the pocket at your left hip.

Market Exchange

And of course, there must be mention of the financier, the accountant in his shiny Glenmore spats and four-piece Geraldelli suit who dipped into the show every so often to check the books and intimidate Plug. He was no bad guy, just a man doing a job, feeding his family. Just a man believing in show-business, the pristine quality of entertainment. He worked for Angus Payton. So much so that the name Angus Payton made him sweat along his receding hairline, made his own name irrelevant.

My image has him walking across the backyard, grey balance books in hand, worried about the mud and grime. Cigar smoke from the mouth of Payton would still be lingering on his coat, in his hair. His thoughts would be about his favourite night-club in Chicago and the waitress who promised him a tumble next time he came through town. He would have around $34.76 on him. He would be considering where he will eat tonight, never having been through Sheboyagan before, worried that it will be bad food and he will have to leave most of his dinner untouched. He would wonder if Plug will ever pay back the two dollars he borrowed three months ago. He would be thinking of Plug's scent, his sweaty beer smell, and the way he chews and chews that repugnant snuff. He would be thinking about how the line-ups at the bank are getting longer and longer.

He would not be thinking about calouses. He would not be thinking about the sideshow performers who draw the crowds who pay the money that Plug will hand over to him to be deposited. He would not be thinking of the crowds, how close they stand to each other. He would not be thinking about the ground churned up by so many feet, some bare.

He always stepped into the red wagon with a impatient sigh.

Logistics

Wilder and his favourite assistant cook headed down the hill to the Illinois River outside Peoria to snag some bullheads for supper. Snow still splayed against the north side of the valley, but on the south side crocuses were in bloom and the dirt breathed a warm muddy whisper. The road wound its way to the swollen river through bald pasture and bluffs of poplar. The walk was much longer than they expected, the distance misleading because of the winding road and the clear spring air.

Wilder was tired already and it was only just past noon. He seemed to be the show's only connection with the real world. First thing in the morning he had to find wood for the stoves. Then he rode into town to barter for day-old bread and went door-to-door in the country south of town to find eggs, flour and milk. Today he also managed to buy a crate full of garlic. He was pleased with that and had begun to alter his menu plans to accommodate the garlic. His hands still smelled of it.

He had a gun on his hip in case they saw any small game—grouse or rabbit, maybe a Canada goose. The pistol sat oddly on his hip and he put his hand on it nervously from time to time as if to make sure the smooth metal hadn't transformed into a demon or that it hadn't shifted to point into his belly. Guns made him jumpy and he was sure some day one was going to betray him. It was inevitable.

Once they found the river's edge, Wilder set the gun aside so he could sit comfortably with the fishing line trailing out into the current. The river was high but apparently not as high as it had been. Silty dead grass covered the bank and hung in limp bunches in the saplings. Chunks of granular ice floated in the brown water. But the sun was strong and fired through the cottonwood that arched over the bank, pressing warmth against the fabric on Wilder's knees. The stiffness in them softened, let out a breath.

The helper splashed in the water a ways down the shore, scooping up plump crayfish and hellbenders for the pot. When he had a bucketful he came and put his line in too. They caught a handful of sunnies quickly, the flat green-gold coins flopping on the shore next to them. The sun had moved half-way down the cottonwood branch when Chup had a big strike. The line jerked out and whipped back and forth. Wilder knew it was a pike and smiled as the young fellow struggled to pull the line in.

Wilder hired Chup after he was tossed from the set-up crew where they thought he was retarded. Didn't take Wilder long to realize he was mute. After going to the menagerie workers to find a proper name for him and some basic Hindi to use, Wilder set him to work in the kitchen. Chup gave Wilder a jar of peaches in gratitude and, after watching Wilder move about the kitchen car for a few days, imitated his every move. Wilder had to instruct him to go ahead and use the two fingers Wilder was missing.

The fish at the end of the line was a big one, a good eighteen pounds, and came glaring and thrashing to the shore. Chup turned to Wilder for help. Wilder waded up to his knees and reached to hook his fingers in the pink gills. But the fish lurched, arched up, and snapped at his hand. The barbed teeth met exactly where Wilder's two missing fingers would have been, then splashed back into the water. Wilder grinned and wagged a good finger at the fish's alligator snout, "Aha, fooled you again, you devil." He stooped and heaved it up on shore where Chup clubbed it with a stick of driftwood.

That fish was not yet cleaned when Wilder's rod bent and pulled him up from his slumber. It too was a big one but this time slow and heavy, forcing Chup to hold on to Wilder's waist as he dragged the line up. Wilder loved that time when he waited for the fish to show, loved to imagine its grandeur, its mammoth dimensions. This time imagination fell short and a massive knobby back floated to the slow surface of the river. "A sturgeon!" Wilder shouted to Chup. They dove frantically to find hand-holds to guide the monster onto land. Dirty water rushed against their legs and into their boots, stunning nerves with cold. The great fish bent to one side, sending Chup staggering to regain his feet on the slick river bottom. Straining waist deep they finally hugged the sturgeon against their chests and hoisted it up onto land.

The fish rolled against the cottonwood, its skin in gnarls like the bark. It wheezed and lay still, finally resigned, Wilder and Chup on top of it, panting. They looked up and silly grins spread across their faces. They thumped each other's soggy shoulders as they stood to look at their prize.

Pale brown and whorled, its back had a ridge of horns running head to tail. It was prehistoric, mouth sucking and twitching with whiskers. Its eyes gleamed back black and intelligent. Snout to tail it was a good foot taller than Wilder.

Finally Wilder could make Jojo proper *baliki*. Full bellies all around. And caviar? Wilder ran his hand down the silvery belly. And caviar! The soft salty pellets were already watering Wilder's mouth. Salted and smoked the fillets would last four days. Four days of provisions. Four days of meals planned just like that. That's all Wilder ever asked. Four days.

Concessions

One of the candy butchers went insane on a Thursday night in Milwaukee. That evening he had gone into the crowd like normal, selling candy and making change from a cloth apron. But after the show he disappeared. They found him the next morning, sobbing in a bin of garbage, candied popcorn stuck in his hair and paper cuts on his face and hands.

He kept blubbering. "All those mouths, hundreds of mouths in the stands, all of them, opening, shouting, teeth and tongues and breath and spit, and all of them, all those mouths, eating, eating, eating, eating eating eating eating eating eating eating eating, chewing and grinding and munching and chomping and biting and slurping and smacking and drooling and swallowing and gulping whole and I couldn't keep up and I kept giving them food from my tray until it was gone and then from my pockets and then from my own mouth I would disgorge and the kids lapping it all up and then that was gone and I'd give them food from myself from me do you understand from my body I'd tear off a chunk and they'd grab it up and stuff it in their mouths still yelling more more more and I'd tear out more of my belly my thighs my arms my neck tearing off more more until I was almost gone and a fat kid stood in front of me screaming more more more and my empty hand descended to his mouth and he swallowed it all and there was nothing left of me nothing left they had eaten it all all the candy popcorn all the taffy all the caramel apples all the coca-cola and goobers and licorice and rock candy and ice cream and lemonade and lion cookies they had eaten it all and they had eaten all of me and all I could see was the last mouth, that huge last mouth, the cheeks puffed, the soft ribbed palate, the quivering pink tonsil, that huge last mouth gaping to devour me, to swallow me whole so there was nothing left, nothing, nothing at all, the dark throat, that last wet descent . . ."

The candy butchers were a tenuous lot, the most transient of the show workers, coming and going quickly, hard to come by. They took this one away in a burlap sack and hired another on the spot. Jojo stood to one side, muttered under his breath just loud enough for a few to hear, "Duas tantum res anxius optat, panem et circenses."

The new fella whooped and scampered away to tell his friends. The show didn't bother learning his name either.

Consumption, Staples

The World's Biggest Cheese! It was a coup.

Hauled in from London, Ontario, weighing no less than 2 tons, made from over 1,000 litres of clover-fed Holstein milk, needing an entire train flatbed to transport, it was stored in a custom-made cooled glass-sealed wagon, needing constant attention, and drew 500 viewers a day for three weeks until it spoiled completely and fed 700 hogs for two days. The heavy rotten milk smell lingered in three Ohio counties for over a month. Finally, an early snow seemed to disperse it but people still talk about it.

It was a mild sweet cheddar.

Outside Janesville we found a missing horse with its throat sliced, flanks and back efficiently cut away into steaks and roasts, heart, liver, tongue, balls, all taken. The ravens had little left.

It was a dray horse named Brady.

Revelation

Like a heavy slap to the face, the freakshow car jerked to a halt and we lost our feet, catapulted to the front of the car and tumbled to the floor. Papers and shattered dishes flew on top of us. Miraculously, no one was seriously hurt in our car except Earle who got a deep cut over one eye on the corner of a table. It wasn't until we scrambled out and looked down the length of the train that we realized the extent of the accident. It was during the summer tour of '97 and the entire train had derailed on the outskirts of Akron.

We all feared rail accidents, heard from other carnies horrible stories of massive derailments. Especially on the rougher tracks the fear hovered at the back of our minds, even the veterans prayed for the arrival whistle, prayed in horror over the wavelets that spattered their coffee, prayed white-knuckled for escape from this long metal coffin.

The wash of relief at our own survival had hardly passed and we were already running madly trying to catch injured horses and put out fires. Alive! we were alive and the air tasted salty like skin! Slowly, agonizingly, car by crumpled car, the damage mounted. Only the last nine cars were spared. The engine, coal car, and the twenty-one cars following were scattered at various angles: some flipped, some on top of others, some well off the track dug into the blasted earth. Wagons from the flatbeds had been tossed hundreds of feet to land and roll to a stop. Many had split like ripe fruit, spilling out the pulp of dead and dying animals or the twisted bodies of half-dressed handlers. Horses ran around with one or more snapped legs and long deep gashes in their sides. Limp bodies, dead or moaning or staring wide-eyed in shock, were being carried out and set in a row on the grass. Trapped voices called, some comforted and assuring, some shrill and panicked.

On the count of three all of us freaks heaved against the side of a box-car, tipping it just enough that Thsk could get under and unhitch a door so four bruised men could slide out. They dusted themselves off and followed along with us.

Earle called Casey's name again and again, wishing his voice matched his frame. His hands trembled. I realized then how alone I was, the Ghost Lady floating free, and yet I craved nothing but the touch of earth or to curl inside someone like they were home. My feet stopped an inch from the ground no matter how hard I pressed myself down.

Four tigers darted confused, dazed orange whips, a wind swept fire through the tall brome grass next to the tracks. And then in a single liquid swoop they rippled up a tall elm, perched there, wide-eyed, licking wounds. One, succumbing to internal injures, fell with a thump to the ground. It bounced and came to rest, its white belly hair stained pink with blood. Even the magic of tigers was not enough to escape. Even that powerful spell became obsolete.

A knot of men tended to an injured woman lying on her belly. They turned and pleaded with us, many of them talking at once, but we couldn't understand, "idhar ao . . . oooooooaaaa, kharab, kharab! . . . hakeem?" Jojo and King stayed with them while we went on. We heard them wail behind us and turned to see their brown arms raised skyward.

In a rush, Casey appeared and catapulted into Earle's arms. They cried and petted the backs of each other's heads. Exhausted with fear, they sat down in the gravel together, legs and arms sprawling. Casey fussed over Earle's cut and we moved on. Was there no end to the cars? The size of the show was never more shocking. How much flesh could there be? Were this many attractions possible?

Remarkably, only one elephant had been killed. For all their size they seemed like they would blow apart with an impact, their thick hips and shoulders already strained to the limit with the improbable mass of their knobby heads. The oldest female, Charosho, had been in the front of the car and had been crushed by the rest as the car bucked off the tracks and came to a skidding halt. All the manacles had been cut and the surviving elephants wandered in a circle around the body of Charosho. Their trunks were raised in alarm, as if looking for an adversary, sniffing the wind for a danger that had come and gone already. We all stopped and stood, the chaos receding, stood outside the ring of elephants, our postures defensive and watchful, and mourned our own and theirs.

LADIES AND GENTLEMEN, BOYS AND GIRLS OF ALL AGES, WELCOME TO THE GREATEST SHOW ON EARTH.

Typography

The show's influence leaked into the early hours of morning, onto the clean streets with ads that plastered every fence and store window. Scenes emerged and dissipated while, alone in our bunks, we slept or drank ourselves into a stupor. Dramas developed only vaguely connected to the glamour of the day's performance.

Four a.m. and the dim light waits, poised to spill out. The tack spitters stand impatient, their breath puffing white into the sharp air. Tag blows on the paint but the air is muggy and it is taking a long time to dry. A tub-size vat of grey glue boils and plops on the wood stove with the tacker's buckets stacked near. The lithographer stands over the artist's shoulder, used to this fickleness but still impatient. The lith machine hunkers in the corner waiting to spin off 2000 copies of this new poster. The specs came in late last night and Tag can't believe the pace.

He brushes lightly along a line of pink, the underside of an aerialiste's arm, hoping the botch of black ink underneath won't show through. The wild wide-eyed faces in the poster stare back at him, waiting to be slapped up on storefronts and fences all over Bloomington. But maybe the elephants should be darker. Tag finds advertising humans very difficult, prefers inanimate subjects. Give him cans of peaches or cough syrup any day. Faces, he has trouble with faces. Should he take out that sad looking clown?

The six tackers laugh loudly, startling Tag. The shortest is standing nose to adam's apple with another, challenging him with mock bravado. Most of them smoke, the last ragged remnants of a fag held gingerly between their thumbs and middle fingers. One of the six has a deformed upper lip and his hair is thin and patchy. He seems to be fearful of his inclusion in the team, standing a few inches further away from the center of the group with his hands deep in his pockets. He laughs at the others' antics but does not dare to enter the banter. They all wear thin wool jackets and their shoes are split and gaping, showing the odd toe or heel. Their brushes are stacked on the stairs to the wagon. The smell of the glue makes their noses run.

The poster is a panorama of circus rings. In the far left ring, the freakshow is represented by three figures: a giant, a bearded lady, and a pin-head, all standing at attention as the elephants thunder by. Tag dips his finest brush to darken the beard. Dabs a few times to make the pinhead's skin darker. He is leaning over with his face just a few inches from the paper. The thumb of his painting hand rubs against his chin, a smudge of black on the thumb rubs onto his chin just under the left side of his mouth.

Nervously his tongue flicks over his lips, his tongue travels down, licks the black paint. He tastes fear. Swallows and leans closer.

Coincidence

The winter of '97, four of the sideshow performers hooked a job in Chicago at the Globe at 300 State St. and learned to love the smell of hogs. The Ghost Lady, the Singing Cherub, Jojo the Dog-Faced Boy and King Sirrah headlined while the rest of the sideshow wintered in Baraboo. Only the best were hired by the dime museum because, being stationary, they had to draw on a limited market. Chicago, drunk on its own industry, craved release, and a wild night at the museum cabaret became the thing to do.

Work took up seven days a week for the performers but there were the odd spring afternoons when they walked out to River Hills to picnic and swim in the lake. During these afternoons, slip had time to watch the others, to learn their eccentricities and secret charms. The Ghost Lady and slip grew a strong gravitational pull, spun slowly around each other, sometimes swinging wide but always drawing back, sitting close, cuddled with slip's head resting in her lap, or standing with Rebecca's hands on each of slip's shoulders. Not mother and child, although those little things, how to get rid of fleas, where to find shoes that didn't cause sores, those boosts a mother would give, were part of their gravity.

The four of them would move across most landscapes with the woman and child walking slow while the other two ranged ahead or off the muddy road. Jojo walked in quick spurts, talking to himself in Latin or Russian, his gaze distant and unfocused, and then he would stop, his eyes would dilate and he'd stoop to study an early spring plant-leaf's filaments, an elaborately armoured bug, or a cowering reptile. He wore a light grey fedora to fend off the noon heat. Languages collided in the colouring of an iridescent beetle and left him gasping.

King walked more comfortably. Arcing off the path he'd stop too. A snowshoe hare not four meters away, nose quivering. King wiggled his nose back and then sprinted away, hopping over wild rose and bare raspberry stalks. He carried his violin everywhere, stopping in the middle of an empty potato field to stroke one rasping note. One rasping note in the middle of the buzz and crackle of grasshoppers. In the woods, he'd whistle and coo with his lips pursed. By plucking the high strings he imitated birdnoise, his eyes searching the branches for response.

When he finally returned to the others, he touched their arms. The thoughts that were scrambling around in their heads stilled and they all walked on.

Patronage

Barnum kept in touch with King through the mail. King didn't make a big deal about it. I am not sure he knew how to read. A few times a year a letter would come with Barnum's seal on it and King, non-plussed, would wag off with it tucked in his pocket. We kept tight-lipped about the letters because we weren't sure what the papers would make of this relationship. We knew Barnum wouldn't mind the media trumping a story but King's career could be damaged. Curiosity nearly killed us though and we craned our necks, made every excuse to hang around King just to get a glimpse of one of the letters.

I got a brief look at one of the letters once but only had time to notice the large erratic hand-written signature on the bottom.

But King whisked it off humming and giggling.

There was no telling where King's act began or ended.

Barnum's death in '89 did not seem to affect him. We broke the news to him but the scratchy violin response did not carry any sorrow. If anything, King smiled knowingly and walked taller with the news bubbling on his lips. "Barnumbarnumbarnumbarnumbar . . ." he'd repeat, over and over like a drum roll.

Recognition

A precise stroke of black over the eyebrow. Once, twice, the touch of a burnt match tip at each end to lengthen. Close, close, almost touching the mirror. The perfect length and width. That ideal arch like an Arabic princess. A dab on the eyelid and then a pinky finger to smudge the black in smooth so it didn't crease after a blink.

Slip would sit watching the Ghost Lady put on her make-up before the show. She never turned to look at him directly, instead watched slip's reactions in the mirror, an easier angle, closer at hand to the business of her face. The vials and jars of pink, sandy-beige, tan-tan, grey, indigo, white powders, creams, and lipsticks were reflected on the other side of the mirror. She talked slowly to the mirror, stopping for long intervals to think or keep her face still to apply something delicate. Her concentration went both ways—to the gaunt pale face, the lines and shades it gradually acquired, and to the words that dabbed and brushed the child sitting at her side. Sometimes both at once. An intense concentration like something very important depended upon each stroke. Slip watched the changing face, the real one talking as well as the one, clearer and gazing intently, in the mirror's reflection.

Rebecca strove to accentuate the acute lines of her face, the signs of age, the angles and vertical lines. For drama, she said, for pure drama. The goal was to emphasize the pale skin and hair by contrast and to give the suggestion of a dead or resurrected body. Rather than let on to the normal bodily reaction to piercing, it was better to attribute supernatural circumstances, bloodlessness, and the power of the undead. It worked. Nothing was ever suggested by the talker or the pamphlets, the audience thought they had it figured out, surmised and conjectured, let their imagination loose. Their theories always turned out to be more elaborate than anything the show could construct.

The make-up obscured her bone structure. Her lips and nose became so shadowed and accented that only the vaguest foundation of her face remained.

So she talked to her lips and her nose when she stood there. Talking to them, saying goodbye as they disappeared beneath lip-liner and a dark blush, making comforting apologies.

"Goodbye lips, goodbye nose, goodbye cheeks, goodbye chin. It's best this way, (pause), we'll go out together tonight after all this, (longer pause), someday we'll run away for good."

With a sly grin she'd mutter, "always making it up to myself."

She tsk-ed at herself in the mirror and got up to go backstage.

"Odd to talk about myself back then. Speaking about that young mulatto hot-shot freak back then like this old mulatto albino woman has nothing to do with her. Just like that little thief slip has little to do with the sad Rice you've become. Where will you go after I have told you all I know?"

The sun had swung around so it shone onto the quilt and Rebecca's bare hands. Her audience had not moved since sitting down. Rice lips moved to speak but it took a long moment for a voice to loosen and crackle out, "I would like to find Earle and Jojo, maybe Annie and some of the others. There's always more."

"Oh, but Earle's dead, died in his sleep twelve years ago. You can't go on like this because you know sooner or later there'll be no place to go next. God knows where Annie is. Last I heard her alias' had grown so many that even she couldn't keep track. I have some of her novels you could read."

She gestured and Rice noticed a stack of books tucked under the night-table. They were dog-eared and faded but were free of dust, as if fingered often. "They may be some comfort but books can only help you so much. As for Jojo, well I can tell you exactly what he'd say if he saw you. He'd wait quietly for the dramatic effect and then say, 'there is nothing profound here. Nothing but you. Look at your hands. Look at your scars.' And then he would look into the distance, suck air through his teeth, mutter, 'Forsan et haec olim meminisse invabit.' And he would say no more. You won't find answers in Jojo's enigma. There are places you won't be able to go, Rice. I spent years returning to Dixie's grave. Over and over the gravestone told me who I was but it wasn't what I needed to hear. A gravestone can't give you what you need. It's stone-still, it won't budge, it can't bend with you. All you do is bump against it, brace yourself beneath it, get trapped by its unmoveable epitaph. You've got to find something else."

And then Rice knew it would be the last time. No place to go, no mystery to unravel, no more words to fill the void. Recognition would have to come some other way.

And then Rice knew the freakshow was over.

Origins

What exactly is a ghost anyway? Help me here.
1. Something that is not there but might as well be.
2. That state we strive for but never achieve because we die first. A kind of idyllic state of transparency that would appeal to the faint of heart. The desire to move invisibly through life and yet have the ability to experience the world with the same senses. And immortality too. A stage above monastic life.
3. The ultimate expression of loss.
4. An opportunity for penitance.
5. A slim chance, a grey wisp of hope.
6. A figure in the near distance, blurred or overexposed, that doesn't fit into the normal order of things, throws the composition off.
7. And so, explained away.
8. An after-image clinging to the pupil when an eye closes to its source.
9. The haunting in the all too real.
10. Just at the periphery of vision, either by choice, necessity, or convenience.
11. The refusal to inhabit a body.
12. The forbidding presence in a story that (ephemerally) embodies true feelings of guilt or loss that the main character denies, a denial which proves to be their ruin.
13. A soul refusing the afterworld (or a soul refused by the afterworld).
14. (   )
15. An absence striving to exist despite the efforts of the all-too-present.
16. The shape of chaotic nothingness at the end of an utterance that

Composition

The sideshow hands and helpers were the lowest of the low but we owed them everything. They hauled our props around, they looked out for troublemakers and put their sleek hard normal bodies between us and the crowds, they mingled as ballysticks and shook the crowds when all the ballyhoo in the world wasn't turning them. Dogged, sweating, they arranged our lives. Like thieves, they would make midnight runs to satiate our cravings. Fried zucchini, metaxa, pimento, moist green cigars, a copy of Scott Joplin's "The Maple Leaf Rag" to play far too loud, a new pair of bloomers, ice in July, magic mushrooms, smoked oysters and roquefort, a drugged minister, hot chilies, bottles of milk to remind us of blue sky, a Ouija board, Drambuie. And they would come creeping back into the ring of wagons with their booty tucked under one arm in a gunny sack. All men, but they were polite and gentle, knocking soft and tentative on the door. They had to be perfect; one squawk from one of us and they were out on their butt. They learned to be comfortable around us. Sometimes they even came to feel like they were one of us.

Their perfect bodies mute, unnamed, invisible in their service and, in that silence, a beautiful counterpoint to our staged glamour, our shouting introductions, our deformities. I took many as lovers, wonderful lovers, quiet and servile, tireless and ever-so-careful.

The young man comes back in with a plate of sliced cheese and pickles. The Ghost Lady smiles up at him, "Rickey here is the second son of Greb, one of my favorite hands. He takes care of me and eases my loss you know." Wink. He leaves as quietly as he comes.

They were always discreet, always polite and, best of all, took rejection well. I can't stand a man who pouts. Or worse, gets nasty when I throw him out on his ear. They were men apart from mankind, a new breed, evolved from the special conditions of the sideshow. Wish I could reproduce that now. Ah, the hands. I sure do miss having all of them.

Topography

But I am wandering. The circus routes were smooth arcs and angles. I just jab my finger at the map here and there as I remember. But of course the slip of old knew the routes, spent hours poring over them.

That's not what you're looking for, not something on a map or in a schedule, not place names and dates. I'm trying to tell you the things behind the names, slip, in the blank spaces between towns, in the terrible silence between shows.

In Carthage, Missouri, the King was whipped to an inch of his life for dragging a stick along a white man's picket fence. And slip pulled him by his armpits a mile and a half to Wilder's wagon. And slip was nine. King left criss-crossed red streaks across slip's belly and chest. One inch of welt equalling about 500 feet. The distance didn't mean anything anymore. The scale, the symbols didn't work anymore. Salt in wounds.

The cartography of your life, slip.

Gravity

A pickpocket earned free movement through the grounds. There was an unspoken rule that the only marks were towners. No performer or hand feared for their wallet or pocket-watch. The circus was past its heyday, everyone knew the managers had to find ways to pay for salaries, feed, and the trains. Jago and slip took a cut of the pot and the rest Plug chuted into the manager's car where Angus sat poring over numbers and countless pieces of paper. Normally, slip got $1 a week for cherub cuteness and earned another $2-3 dragging the midway, sieving through the bigtop and the sideshow grind. The gig was to act lost, looking for parents.

Somehow, inconceivably, the little cherub thief had acquired a heightened sense of moral conduct. Fortunately, slip had reasoned it through with Jojo, settling on the fact that being lost wasn't an outright lie. Despite slip's insurmountable naiveté, an attention to right and wrong hovered over slip's every action.

The draw was a dramatic and frantic pointing toward a distant couple: "There they are!!!" A wide vest pocket waited to stow the take. Often the mark discovered the items missing while slip was still perched in his arms but never once did anyone catch on and suspect such an innocent child.

"Ah, my little forlorn waif, my little artful dodger, come to papa and tell him what you've found," Jago would croon, more interested in the artistry than the coins and jewelry.

In between shows slip would wander about asking and demanding, watching the lion act practice or silently taking in a conversation between aerialists.

Not at all conscious of status, slip marched right up to the high-wire acts and the arrogant show-girls, shaking hands and asking where they were from. These performers were mostly Italian or South American and would tell slip of their homeland. They spoke little English, verging back and forth between languages. The performers laughed when they heard slip's piercing voice. They'd shout, "Sing, sing, a beneplacito, please sing, bambino" and clap when slip came scurrying into the tent.

The menagerie hands took a shine to slip and Jabal, the super, hoisted slip up to ride beside him as he directed the shuffled pens, the feeding and watering. Jabal was old and slow. His pinto horse carried him everywhere and his eyes were like an elephant's, light brown and deep like soft mahogany. To the menagerie hands, slip was the *chhota chor*, the child-thief, but the sharp "ch" sound turned loving in their mouths. They were Turks and Sikh, and their shouts and banter swirled around the serene instructions of Jabal. They called the super *Aga* and watched him closely as he expertly checked an elephant's ears for mites.

Standing slack-jawed, slip would watch the clowns who practiced off to the side of the rings and stayed in their own rowdy part of the grounds. I always found them spooky, got nervous whenever one came over to talk, leaning close like he was telling a secret. The one with the black-eyed susan, near gone, seemed to be telling slip his last requests. He talked breathless and guilty when he thought no one was watching.

"Ah, slip it must be slip, come closer and hear me die in your arms closer my whispering from fear slipping through my painted lips like a moth or my wishes closed overtop by canvas and one drooping orange flower is all slip a light at the end a tunnel of fanfare a black swirling me away these potions and powders tucked deep in a left lung when whispered poison wilts your tender ears licked into revulsion slip jump jump from the burning building into my desperate net failing us both mock i am mock humanity slip don't you see i want to be inhuman like a poster or an insane painting tell me slip tell me my face is peeling tell me my skin is dissolving slip take the smallest sip of my thoughts let it tipsy your easy gaze let me trouble your laughing sleep slip come closer to death and tell me you love me tell me my whispered words back tell me i exist so i can cease" he gulped air threatening to stop, "and bottle myself in your mouth a swig a last gasp slip my act is expiration turned over upsidedown death i cannot say it anymore than a coming back to life over and over like make-up and i whisper to death every night backstage wondering then when the paint stays and the show will walk slowly by me without me moving without a whisper to no one slip will you see me then will you see me then when i am dead again."

Metamorphosis

If a hand tilts toward a window lit with a flannel afternoon, tilted palm out, fingers away, if the hand is used to grasping paper gripped tight and accustomed to the anxious rub of the worn upholstery of old busseats, if the hand gently raps on a door to a room overfilled with conviction, if the hand is thin, the fingers thin as pens, the fingers poised to record themselves into being, if the hand is tattooed with denial, if the hand has rested in another thin hand, this one pale and pocked with holes, if the hand once convinced now becomes limp, loosens its grip, unhinges and tilts toward a window vaguely lit, if the hand is tilted palm out, fingers away, if the hand reaches for this flannel afternoon, there! in this instant, time is set free from whatever binds it and the hand becomes the hand of a little thief, becomes a hand opening to steal the sun.

The Exotic Idyllic

It was the habit of the show to portray itself as harmonious and sedate. Images of the comradery, the troupe spirit, the close-knit family of freaks was good for publicity.

It was a crock.

Thsk was absent—even more than his tiny frame warranted—not part of a happy family at all. He kept to himself and communicated only as much as necessary. Brief hellos and business matters. Arrangements. Choreography. He sat for hours playing the rickety old fortepiano the show carted every night from his wagon to the stage for performances. He claimed the instrument was an antique, formerly of the court of King William IV and a favorite toy of Beethoven. He babied it, worrying and fussing over it every time a hand tried to hoist it too casually, scolded and stroked its warm finish. The fortepiano was his companion day and night, on and off stage. His chubby hands became suddenly, inexplicably elegant when they began to move over the stained yellow keys. All night sad bars of Debussy and Grieg came floating out from his isolated little world. High, lilting sonatas sent wafts of melancholia across the grounds. Wilder brought him jars of artichoke hearts when he missed dinners but hardly a word passed between them. A cocoon of music grew around him.

Thsk was with the show longer than any of us. The midwest circuit was his one and only. One act, one route, year after year. Unusual for a freak but Thsk had talent, real talent, and was good enough to call his shots. He was the toast of Chicago and the kingpin of the sideshows until one winter when his twin sister in England died. Tashia was her name and they used to write letters constantly, every day a stream of words whose ebb and flow was only affected by the inconsistencies of the post. Letters flew like arias across the Atlantic, orchestrating a familial bond between New World and Old.

Thsk longed to return to England but London had exiled him. Rumours had ignited that Thsk (then Reginald) and Tashia were lovers, and Buckingham Palace banished the two performers. To quash the rumours Thsk had to leave. Propriety demanded his departure. With Tashia's career at stake, Thsk did the honourable thing but it was the saddest day of his life. When the liner H.M.S. *Rochester* floated away from the dock on its maiden voyage from London's harbour, its impenetrable hull did not seem nearly strong enough to prevent the tides from flooding in. Salt sea sprayed up into their eyes and the continents drifted them apart.

But the letters, heartfelt masterpieces of eloquent emotion and intellectual dialogue, created a floating bridge of words. Each twin anticipated exactly what the other would write, the other trying to surprise with new insights but never straying far from the intimate familiar words that tied them together. The letters were Thsk's grappling hook to England, back to the elegance of London, back to the quiet afternoons in Hyde Park and the peaceful tea-times with his sister, back to the small brick house in Lambeth he dearly missed. The midwest seemed crude in comparison, and Thsk finally decided not to acknowledge its existence, instead surrounded himself with London. The only thing he discovered in America that was of any consequence was artichoke hearts. Imported artichoke hearts. He thanked Wilder for that and went back to his room to write.

After a long cold wet spell in London, Tashia fell ill and died of respiratory problems. A thin trail of letters reported her illness, then stopped, and Thsk's hands trembled over the stack of mail he had pony expressed from Baraboo. Nothing. One month, two. Four. Finally word from a cousin and even then, Thsk wrote angry letters demanding explanations for their outrageous lies. He retreated further. Except for the audiences, Wilder became his only connection with the outside. Even there, on stage, Thsk's playing seemed to close in on itself, the music hidden within the pads of his fingers. Dvorak was fire without a source, Mussorgsky's "Pictures at an Exhibition" berated the audience.

But still he wrote, as much or more than before. Letters by the sackful sent across the ocean on steamers and liners, faithfully addressed to Tashia, arriving in London only to be tossed in the dustbin.

Thsk wrote on, volumes of poetry and stories, anecdotes and details of his day, essays expounding the virtues of the monarchy and diatribes on the moral degeneration of mankind, notations on a burgeoning sonata, wails from the longest loneliest of nights.

And Thsk wrote on, the music spewing out over the Atlantic, searching for that perfect curve of ear.

A Theory of Two

"There's not a thing in this world you can't fake." Jojo was near drunk and had led slip into the forest near the reservoir. Elms drifted against the wide periphery of stars. No moon and in the woods the dark took over, left only sound, touch (the scrape of bark on forearm, slap of leaves), and heartbeats. And then just Jojo's voice.

"There is nothing in the world you can't fake. There is nothing in the world that is not fake. It's all a gaff. 1829. My father's village, named Doroga by my great grandfather, was convinced by a crazy woman to stockpile water because a drought was coming. Sort of like Noah in reverse. No drought came but my father's pottery wheel was never still. The drachmas poured in. The clay dug in until his fingernails fell off. The crazy woman later became my mother. Part of me thinks men want to reclaim the primitive, some ideal perfection of nature; yet part of me thinks it's a matter of mastery, transcending nature, because nature terrifies us to the point of denial, invention even. Darwin invented. 'A devil's chaplain might write on the clumsy, wasteful, blundering, low, and horribly cruel works of nature.' Darwin. How that pious fraud must hate this world to turn it into an economy. On the boat over my family had to pretend I was badly burned and covered me in gauze or they would have never taken me on the boat. It was the first time I ever understood that an iceberg was possible. Did you know that if it wasn't for water's unique property of being lighter in solid state than in liquid, life would have never developed on this planet? Ellis Island seemed to float towards us, not the boat towards the island. The New World, for all its love of freaks, would never allow one like me to enter as a citizen. Customs, customer, costume; they're all one. My father brought a sack of clay over from Russia, hoping to mix it with the soil of his new home. But we never owned our own land and when he died, the clay went into his grave. Water? Could water unite us all? I am practicing how to lap water. It is very difficult. Have you ever tried it? No, curl your tongue more. I nearly drowned the first time I tried. The only thing consistent about faking is the need to progress, make the spectacle more complicated, surprising. Agh, I have a killer itch, could you . . . a little farther down, ya, ya, ya, aaaaaaaa-aaaa . . . perfect. I am a tenant in a condemned building who is about to be evicted. Have you ever tried thumping your arm when someone scratches your back? It's really quite satisfying, makes it feel like you are doing it all yourself. Although you can recycle the fraud too. People have no memory for diversions. Politicians can pull the same crap over and over, no one remembers. Command us to bear false witness. No watchdog can keep up with the expediency of fraud. Bow down before them, serve them. I live in a house of bondage and it is falling down around us."

Orchestration

LAAAAADIES AND GENTLEMEN, BOOOOOYS AND GIRLS OF AAAAALLLLLLLL AGES, WELCOME (a huge sweep of the arm) UNDER THE BIG TOP.

And the litany began once again. And the show began again, each performer putting on their circus faces, each face frozen in different ways, and each with a growing sense of apprehension under the mask. Each night the invocation led the audience on with a little less conviction. The lion tamers, the riders, the jugglers, the highwire and trapeze artists, the strongman, the clowns.

And then, off to the side, the freakshow. The spiel of each fantastic discovery, the freaks' hardworking families, conjecture on the origins of their afflictions, traumas during birth, planetary misalignments. The crowd, all those faces, the freaks could barely see over that distance, and the grinding spiel bellowed out across the grounds over and over, until we couldn't hear it any more. But hearing, listening past the bluster and pomp, could turn the sacred into the blasphemous, the innocent into the insidious, comfort to exile, magic to bare-knuckled manipulation. The show sang and roared with expectation, the audience, the performers, all waiting for the ringmaster or the talker, waiting for paradise, the unbelievable, the reassuring chaos, waiting to be transformed.

WELCOME TO THE GREAAAAAAATEST SHOW ON EARTH.

Twenty-four horses carried 24 dogs gripping 24 banners in their teeth. Out and around they paraded as Anthony the ringmaster sends proclamations into the crowd, sealing the contract with the waxy sanctity of words. And promising more. The crowd leaned in, searching for the magic beneath the whirling pins, beneath the sequins and masks, beneath the flashing eyes, painted faces, measured gaits. They leaned in looking for magic—for love, for passion, for sublime drama. They leaned in looking for a covert glance between the lion-tamer and the long-legged trapeze artist, looking for murderous jealousy between the jugglers, hoping for wild insanity in the eyes of the clowns. They leaned in already lost in the vision, already given themselves up to delicious torment. They leaned in, searching for salvation.

And slip knew every dazzling moment, every crescendo, every startling display. Choreography was slip's tool, the dance interpreting itself, the wallets and purses of the crowd small bundles of revelation.

"Beccabeccabeccabeccabecca . . ." The voice of little slip falls out of the attentive silence of Rice with a whimper. Head in boney hands, says over and over, "becca beccabeccabecca . . ."

Finally, in a whoosh, "Give me a day, just one, but a whole day, all of it, give me all of it, give me it all back, every bit, not a special day, not anything special, just a normal day, but everything from it, all of it, can you, can you please Becca?" Rice's head slowly lowers, tips into her lap, breath held.

"I can try Rice, but to tell you everything'd take a whole day then, or more, probably more, to tell you a whole day detailed and slow. It'd probably take me a day just to tell you what you see the instant you wake up in the morning. But I'll try. This ghost's got nothing but time anyway. A day will have to fly into my head before I can even try. Let me keep going in bits and then maybe a whole day'll put itself together. You see I'm trying to make an even shape from all this slip, believe me. I know you need the package of your life placed back in your hands. But it ain't so easy, life ain't even, it's bumpy and everywhere and ragged and you can only collect it neat and easy with lies. I had enough of lies. But maybe that's what you want. You want lies, Rice?"

"No. No, that ain't memory then."

"Well, sometimes, sometimes it is."

"OK. OK, you can lie, Becca . . ."

". . . but don't tell me when you do."

Fame

One night slip flew back to the sky again. It was a supper-to-supper daylight stint so the set-up was overnight and the gate wasn't until the next day. Fitful practice-work leapt at the edges of the backyard and springboards thumped as slip mixed among the clowns searching for the one who had whispered, the one with the black-eyed susan on his lapel. But he was nowhere to be seen.

By late evening, slip ended up in the empty bigtop; the canvas sighing, the center and sidepoles swaying slightly, guy wires humming with the tension. The stands swung wide and converged to hold the three rings in place. Slip's bare feet shuffled through the sawdust toward a bright red and blue ball that had been left in the center ring. Stepping into the ring, slip looked closer at the wood pilings that marked the boundaries of the show. In between the cuts and scars, names came clear from the wood, carved with a knife or pick: Joe Granvile, J.L. Manteia, Floyd McKennon, Jiggers, Krafchenko. Circus performers, doing a second rate circuit, trying to leave an imprint when they retired, after they disappear from the limelight. But who would see these except other circus performers? On the center pole too, even more densely, names scratched on top of the other: Barry Gray, Memzi K. Lily, Sophia Fevvers, Debbie Lou, Hazard LePage. Some burned on in streaky black smudges, some in white and red paint: Willie Ingram, Chaska Fellows, Bob Goldsack, James Hardy, Madame Carolista, Dixie Wilson, Bobby Kork. As the evening faded, slip read higher and higher on the pole until the names dissolved in the dark wood above.

Straining to catch the last of the signatures, slip saw a large bird on a platform at the very top of the center pole. Maybe a raven or a peregrine. It moved awkwardly and slip wondered whether the bird was nesting or caught accidentally inside the tent. Instead of answering, the bird spread its wings and dropped in a slow curve. Achingly slow, the empty bigtop-time stalled, and slip saw that it was not a bird at all but a man in spangled white pants, a black derby, and wide plush wings. A man with wings. And slip was plucked up lightly as a lark, strong hands gripping under armpits. Ground and sawdust drifted below. In slip's left ear, "Awake, my friend, awake!"

Up, up slip rose dizzy in a return to the sky, the stained canvas still holding the warmth of the day's sun. Below, the concentric rings and stands turned into an abstract design, hieroglyphs in the dust.

The bird-man hovered, then plopped slip down on the platform planks. His wings were burnished silver and slip was surprised at the wizened old face under the absurd bowler hat. After gaining his balance slip took in the clutter scattered over the platform. Square in front, near the center pole, a neat table with two chairs, a lace-edged tablecloth, and a clay vase filled with star-gazers. A large weather-stained upside-down globe of the world and a crude porcelain wash basin sat on the edge of the platform. Boxes filled the rest of the space, the nearest of which contained nothing but small oranges.

"Awake, my little cherub, open your eyes and talk with Win a while. Tell your guiding angel what you are looking for." But slip was stunned. "Oh, come on, tell me I haven't come all the way from Istanbul to land with a band of turkey-footed dolts with no ambition, no grace, no ideals. Let me tell you about the Orient Express, that motionless place festooned with stories, that place on wheels grinding across history, across worlds, where magic made me live. Let me tantalize with mangoes and sugarcane from the jungles of Siam, let me dazzle with crystal and jade from the cliffs of Tibet, let me comfort with silk from Manchuria and seal fur from the ice-flows of Kamchukta."

He was a showman through and through. But slip had been around the show long enough to know desperation lingered behind his spiel—like he was bartering for his life at the same time as he was showing off all those trinkets.

Desperation was shared by almost all of the performers. The turn of the trick, the sale, the blow-off, that was all they had. Their lives were built around the ability to hold the audience's attention, to grab those gazes and make them stick. The spiel made slip feel oddly comfortable. Birds of a feather.

Pleading, Win swooped around the small platform popping objects and fruit into slip's arms. A cold red juice ran down one forearm and there were indeed silks and furs. Trunks and boxes lay half opened and scattered across the floor. One near slip's foot had a collection of seashells, a few feet off a square cage filled with straw held some unseen animal making a high-pitched squeak.

But Win appeared in front of slip again, looking for attention. Dark-skinned and wiry, he seemed to move faster than eyes could follow so slip was several times startled to find him somewhere else or suddenly near. The man-bird's voice was practiced at spieling—had that run-on rhythm and dramatic inflection that slip recognized. Across the platform, slip's eyes were drawn to the point at which wing met shoulder blade, looking for the gaff. Couldn't.

"Ah, I see I ain't turning ya, am I. Looking like you seen it all." His arms and wings drooped to his sides and he turned and walked over to slip, not with quick flaps and jerks but slow and resigned.

"I'm old and worn out. Thinking of retiring, being a very old man with wings isn't what it used to be. Used to be my wings would get me adoration, awe, a dose of religious fervor. Used to be wings would get me throngs, whispers of devotion, gifts of gold and spices, invitations by presidents, foreign officials, shahs, generals, queens, popes. Used to be wings meant wisdom, other-worldliness, holiness, even blind faith to the point of sacrifice. Used to be the public staggered in the gale of my beating wings."

He stopped for a minute, took a white tablet from a pouch and slipped it under his tongue. "Now there is no god. Now to be a man with wings suspended above a humming crowd means a desire to discover, defeather, drag the freak down to earth. Now I am lusted after—women in fur coats gaze at my crotch, fat men with sweaty jowls finger my plumage, drooling like thanksgiving. Now to survive means giving a peek, a flash of buttock, a glimpse of inner thigh. Now to survive means furtive escapes, never being alone, isolating myself up here, learning how to sell myself with just the right pitch. There is no future for a man with wings. God is no benefactor and myth has left me behind."

A chill crept down from the canvas above. Win's eyes glittered and his wings framed him like a photographer's backdrop. "I am thinking of a tropical retirement. Someplace warm like South America where piety still means something, where magic still has a foot-hold. An old caller told me that on the north coast near Bogotà there still is a piece of paradise. Quiet villages that value honour, peace, where a god can move through the smallest of miracles. That's where I am headed my little friend. No more of this farce, this chicken-feed pay, those low-blow looks, those screaming voices wanting more." He turned to slip and leaned over the edge of the platform. "There may be something I can amaze you with, although it is not of my own design."

Win sat down with his skinny legs dangling over the platform edge and looked down. Slip followed suit. Below, pan lamps were being lit, performers wandered in to practice or to socialize. Slip could not see faces from that distance but realized voices were crystal clear. Each word or grunt, every joke, command, curse, whisper, cough, suggestion, prompt, every bit of gossip, banter, and intimate conversation was funnelled up the tent-sides, landing lightly on slip's ear.

A juggler dropped a pin with a loud "thwack." He slumped, muttered under his breath that he wouldn't go on, this was it, he was giving up, moving back to Albequerque. He slammed down the pins and left. His voice sounded like a final request.

A highwire walker stood on a platform twenty feet below. She said a prayer over and over again; "Hail Mary full of grace, hail Mary full of grace, hail Mary full of grace, full of grace, full of grace, full of grace, full of grace, full of grace, grace, grace, grace, grace, gracegracegracegracegrace . . ." She had a slim child-like voice with a Spanish accent. The words sounded like a whisper over a pillow just before bed, until the prayer broke down, the voice crumbled into tight-lipped bile. Grace folded into itself and then she was silent. Stepped forward.

Slip heard that the sideshow was getting a new bannerline and that most of the performers didn't approve, thought it was wasted on "those freaks." The whispery dry flow of currency, the snap of a new crisp bill, the wet flap of bad blood money floated up to slip.

An aerialist with a voice like a tightrope whispered, "meet me by the water tower after lights out," to a bull hand. The bull hand hustled across the rings to cancel a previously arranged rendezvous with a pony-rider. His voice didn't crack with the guilt, cool liquid already rushing in his veins.

Voices carried the show. Win smiled at the wonder in slip's face, eyes closed, head filling with story.

Sounds slid in from outside the tent, from across the grounds and all the way from town. Sound funnelled through the tent flaps and spiralled up, up into the far reaches where slip crouched. A woman sang quietly to herself in some upstairs bedroom, a lullaby. By the tracks, three kids talked about their dicks, their laughs like zippers, and there was a train coming around the bend. An old woman had just won a ceramic clown at the bottle-throw and it shattered when she chucked it back at the surprised caller.

There was no end to sound. It resounded, accumulated, reverberated, the whole world seemed to wheeze and groan in slip's ears. The clamour built and built until finally slip lurched backwards, fell unconscious into a startled bird's wings.

Conspiracy

Perhaps the show was the dream of Dixie DeHavilland as she lay at rest in a small cemetery surrounded by weeping birches outside Traverse City. At the rushed funeral, slip solemnly placed a cherry pal and a short length of velvet rope on her grave. Sea gulls argued in the cemetery and crocuses bruised beneath our feet. About a dozen of us made it out. The show left no time for mourning or rituals. A cherry pal and a bit of velvet rope. All I could do was set a yellow lily on her empty seat that night as we posed for the voracious crowds. They complained at her absence, mouthing phrases like "money's worth" and "false ads." I was numb.

Before she died she was bedridden for a week and half. This was not unusual for Dixie. It had happened before when her knees gave out or her back spasms got too painful. But this time when I went to see her she said she was having bad bad dreams. I'd sit on the tenuous edge of her bed, the window wide to ease the smell. Dixie told me she thought she was dying, said she was comforted to have somebody to tell stories to while she waited. So I sat there listening to her tell me all about herself. Some true some probably not-so, she would wink at me. Her dreams came tumbling out in place of all the food that had stopped tumbling in. She said that every night in her fitful half sleep, a dark-skinned naked woman came to the foot of her bed. She thought it was an angel. But the angel spoke a strange language, intense, demanding, and clipped, and she couldn't understand what was being asked of her. Dixie shook her head and told me she would look for signs of beckoning—an outstretched hand, a curled finger—but none came. Instead the angel would point at her own muscular chest and shake her fist as if trying to rouse Dixie. White eyes glowed anger and bare feet stomped against the floorboards in frustration. So beautiful towering there at the foot of the bed, Dixie stumbled over her words trying to describe her.

She died on a hot Tuesday evening and they took her away in a flatbed carriage. I wondered whether she had deciphered the language or had touched the angel. I wondered if she finally had a good night's sleep before she died.

But perhaps, perhaps she dreams us as we speak, dreams the circus to life, the dazzle, the trains, the sweets. Perhaps she dreams the sideshow as a haven, as a place to be safe, for a time, from the stones and spit of the street.

As a fat lady from Baton Rouge she had to face a lot of shit. Nothing like unusual dimensions and an odd smell to provoke violence and elicit disgust. While in the show we were looked at in wonder, with a certain respect. We marveled at our own ability to manufacture awe. As the Fat Lady, as Dixie Lane, Dixie was transformed into more than a fat lady. She was the Heaviest Woman on Earth. She could make pop bottles disappear into her cleavage. She had a larger bicep measurement than Casey the Strongman. She had 47 pairs of shoes and delicate feet. She could eat an entire hog at one sitting. She was divine.

Her hasty gravestone read, dixie dehavilland, larger than life, 1870–1899.

Now, in her restless sleep, she rolls over, nestles us freaks safely between her monstrous breasts.

Designation

Long before slip ever set little feet onto the stage, we did a memorable show outside K. C. to a full house. It was like any other show except we saw Plug go running into the audience. He stopped in front of a huge man and through the hubbub of the exiting audience we heard him ask, "How would you like to be a giant?"

The tall man looked befuddled and surprised by the question. "Are you calling me a freak?"

"No, but I could make you one, and famous too. Whaddya say?"

Earle Gideon had never thought of himself as anything but just plain tall. A giant? What did that mean? Earle had a sad countenance, a long drooping chin, eyes like inkwells, and a huge beefy nose holding up fragile-looking glasses. He was too uncoordinated to be much help on his father's ranch but he had started auctioneering at the local market. This small town knew him, had known him since he was a kid, a gangly awkward kid. The town's eyes grew with him so his height wasn't the spectacular thing that Plug saw.

"I'm a good public speaker, maybe I could do some acting."

"Oh hell ya, we'll have you strutting like a star on stage in no time. Come back stage and we'll sign you up a contract on the spot."

Earle looked back outside the tent where the audience wandered into town. He watched their normal sized backs, normal sized pituitary glands, normal sized lives retreating out the tent entrance. That wasn't an audience, those were his neighbours.

"Yes, I will be your giant."

After thirteen years in the grind, as he left the show forever with Casey the Strongman on his arm, Earle looked back toward us, called back as if from a great distance, "Send word if you ever need a tall guy for anything."

Revolution

Those were wild times, slip. Hardly a day went by when we didn't hear of some new discovery, some amazing advancement, some new-fangled luxury device. Sad to say but this Ghost Lady lying here is behind the times nowadays. I don't know what's going on and I've given up trying. I think we all get to that age where new things just don't fit any more, an age where inventions start slipping through the tattered safety nets of our heads.

But back then, back then things were happening that staggered the mind. Electric lights! I couldn't believe it. All those years of kerosene pan lamps and those dim hissing flames and, all of sudden, we had light with the flip of a toggle!

And printing. The tackers were making up more extravagant posters every year. Bright and bold. Images that leapt out and nearly bit you.

The telephone! I could hardly believe my ears the first time. I kept looking around for the person whose voice I was hearing. I was calling from Buffalo to Chicago on one of the first lines to confirm my winter contract with the Kohl-Middleton dime circuit. My head couldn't wrap itself around the idea of Mr. Middleton so far away speaking directly to me. He paid of course. But directly to me! Talking over all those miles! I kept looking past the receiver thinking he was hiding there, tricking me.

And did you know there was a theory that we are all made up of little bits called molecules? Incredible! People walked around in a daze with the idea hanging heavy in their once pristine bodies, with the knowledge that they were made up of the same things as the shit on their shoes. My molecules were the same as some queen's! And that when we died, all these molecules just dissolved back into the dirt. Like into a big soup or stew. We split apart and turn into other things. It was too much for some people. To try and salvage some pride that fella Darwin even invented a theory called evolution—which seems to be just another word for snobbery if you ask me.

Still seeping, that diluted death, that great equalizer lurked on street corners and in the groaning weight of humanity, still gnawed at the edges of streetlight. And so, America invented the spectacle. Invented the audience to fend off death and the smell of rot from all those lurking molecules. A pageant, a story, a statue, organized, to ward off the worms.

And I went to the Professor and I asked him whether we were made up of molecules just the same. He cringed, baby! Cringed and slunk outta there mumbling about me being insane or something! You insane woman! This technology stuff wasn't so bad!

The Image (the image)

The night Win premiered as Michelangelo the Flying Man, the whole show's knees shook. We'd puffed this act to the max, and the survival of the whole show rested on its success. Our jobs hinged on this headliner. We all prayed to a man with wings to win back our audiences.

The Barnum & Bailey was killing us, making inroads across the midwest, swooping in to towns ahead of schedule, rerouting to cut into our path. Some big bucks were flying around to mayors and councilmen to change zoning commitments and permits. The B & B tackers seemed everywhere. The ghost of Barnum shouted from their parades. It was do or die for Sells-Floto. The rivalry had snowballed into an all-out media war between the two circus giants. Full page ads, posters, billboards, bannerlines, wagonsides, flags, handbills, all became soldiers in the war. We were not soldiers but it was hard not to get caught up in the rivalry, in the heat of competition, and some of the younger hands bantered back and forth on the issue, cursing Barnum and shouting, "Viva Floto!" But, except for job security, this struggle of giants did not really interest us much. Market economies and monopolies all seemed unreal and out of reach. Just idle, frivolous talk between deities.

Drawing the crowds was the best job security. And Win was our ticket.

And they descended in throngs to see him. They waited eager for his entrance. His turn finally came and he unfurled himself from a makeshift aviary made of evergreen bows and twine, perched up at the pinnacle of the center pole.

The crowd craned their necks, jaws automatically gone flaccid. Could it be? Could this be an angel?

Finally come to earth? And he was *oh* so sexy. They wanted to make love to him. Every last one of them, even before they saw him, they wanted him. Wanted to own him. Know his secrets. Put words like three wishes into his pouting mouth. Suck them out with their own rough lips. Nothing they saw tonight could disappoint that hunger.

The talker's voice was hushed, apparently awed along with the crowd. A company of horses knelt on cue, bowing down before the spectacle. The butchers even stopped hawking.

"Godspeed," slip whispered, stealing into the midst of the crowd.

Win moved achingly slow, drawing the moment out. Awkward humps behind his shoulders shuddered and slowly rose. A drum-roll burgeoned out of silence, hardly perceptible, sound beginning in the soles of the feet. He now stood at the parapet, the long angular feathers framing his shoulders, silvery tips tapered to his feet. He wore a white wig and a white seamless bodysuit with scattered sparkles around his neck, nipples, and groin. He stood straight, his faced turned down towards the audience with a sad gaze of incomprehension or despair. A blank gaze that could be filled with anything the audience wanted. When he had almost waited too long, he finally stepped forward. Forward into the air. And fell.

He plummeted toward the sawdust and dirt, a stone with his beautiful wings like a comet tail trailing uselessly behind. His sad face unchanged, grew larger, clearer. His descent whined like a violin string and deep in the throat of the audience a sympathy whine grew. God was dead. There was nothing left.

But, at the last possible moment, the wings snapped forward and Win arced into a glide, level, low over the crowd, and then floated up, climbing back toward the tent top.

The crowd hadn't even time to gasp. Had no time to look for gye lines or pulleys. Had no time to disbelieve. He landed on the highwire, balanced, a hint of smile. All that was left of the flight was a feathery gust of air, which eddied and swirled around the audience's faces. The smell was crisp and dusty but comforting like a familiar attic or shelf of knick-knacks.

After he landed there was a slight pause in which the audience considered whether they had been duped or embarrassed. Satisfied, as one, voices roared approval, thundered consent to continue. The breath from the crowd ruffled Win's feathers, sent the highwire swaying.

His wings were unfurled and lit in the full light of the lamps. They glowed to either side of him three times the width of his outstretched arms. In that light, his ribs and spare frame, the worry lines and wrinkles on his face, even the single tear falling from his upturned eye, became visible but no one noticed. No one noticed because the heat of the heaven-sent descent was still warm in their throats. Still trembling their thighs.

Resistance

Earle and Casey the Strongman would meet at the edge of the backyard, back where the crates and barrows leaned against the makeshift snowfence set up to keep kids and thieves clear. They'd stand close together so everybody knew they had fallen in love. Their bodies a proclamation. They leaned into each other's ungainly passion, let loose those certain laughs with the hysterical quivering tag at the end, let a hand stray languidly to touch an elbow, a hip, a chin. They would pass small gifts to each other with sparkling eyes and fidget. The present was always perfect, always inspired, always left the other gaping in amazement, "How did you know?"

Love was an intuitive complicity.

Love made their bodies suddenly small and vulnerable. Those massive flanks turned to jelly. The jutting bristled jaws went slack with the curl of a leering conspiratorial lip. The huge ragged bundles of their hearts beat just as fast as any other love-struck waif. Casey gasped shyly when Earle reached down to stroke his bulging crotch. Clumsiness fell away from them like discarded crutches. The world disappeared like a small room long deserted.

When 600 collective pounds of machismo falls head over heels, gravity becomes an insubstantial theory. The rest of the show tsk-ed and rolled their eyes like it was any other foolish couple. "There go the two young love-ostriches," they'd say. Their voices boomed and leap-frogged to new heights of volume and velocity. Most relationships between show-people become publicity events but this one was ignored by Plug and the managers as if it didn't exist. Public opinion stood brooding, a constant fan and critic, waiting outside the show-grounds.

They wore each other's clothes and they stole delicate kisses behind the canvas bannerline. And the sideshow fell in love with their love, buoyed by its impossibility.

When the show stopped in Niagara Falls that autumn they decided to announce what everybody already knew and arranged a small wedding ceremony. They gathered all the sideshow performers by the falls and the mist pearled in everyone's eye-lashes. The ceremony was complete with a big cake surrounded by peonies and birds-of-paradise studded with gangly sunflowers. The burly flowers drooped, dipping down to brush their shoulders as they took their places. They both wore tails and top-hats borrowed from wardrobe. Earle had been having trouble with his balance and a slipped disc, so he carried a cane to steady himself. The King presided with a large dusty book which turned out to be an old copy of *Tristram Shandy* in the absence of an available Bible. The three of them stood framed by an arbour against the backdrop of the falls; the King, head bowed between, was dwarfed by the towering lovers who stood hand-in-hand, reciting from memory vows they had prepared weeks in advance. The small audience wept. Mostly in happiness, but weeping can turn into all sorts of spillage.

Jojo was best man and looked smashing in a tweed jacket, vest, and spats. He had to steady Earle several times during the ceremony and had to help both men get their rings out of their pillow nests, his smaller fingers taking charge. In her glory, Dixie was maid of honour next to Casey and stood resplendent, wailing and cooing through the whole thing. Her pink frilled dress made her appear the larger cousin of the plump peonies behind her. The rings and bouquet arrived under the care of slip, an obvious choice for ring-bearer and flower girl. Unused to giving jewelry rather than stealing it away, slip frowned in concentration through the whole event.

Then came the climactic kiss, the two behemoths gently tipping toward each other. A mythic kiss, an iconoclastic kiss, an illicit kiss; whatever you wanted to call it, their lips met for a full thirty seconds, and their intimacy deafened.

The audience rushed up and hugged them both, standing on tip-toe to reach each ruddy blushing cheek. Thsk approached them and was ceremoniously lifted up between the two and soundly smooched on both cheeks. His melancholia broke for an instant and he smiled in the midst of a rumpled huff.

King pranced around shouting "do you take, do you take, do you take . . ." with slip shouting "do it again, do it again, do it again . . . " alongside.

The Horseshoe Falls thundered applause.

Piles of Wilder's baking and jugs of ale waited back at the grounds and the wedding party sang loud marching songs and cried long into the night. Earle and Casey slipped out into the blinding bright moonlight and just stood alone, mesmerized for a long while. Happiness had slipped through the gate, snuck through the press and lunge of the gawking crowds, hopped the velvet rope to place itself in their palms. They felt, standing there, that maybe they could follow that messenger back out of this place and never return.

The Idyllic

Jojo and Earle enjoyed an ongoing animosity that straddled the rude but rarely exceeded the curt. The hard feelings had evolved from a nasty drunken incident near Mitchell. The show was whipping through South Dakota and had stopped for a few days off. Days off on the prairie meant a dereliction of senses along with the dereliction of duties.

In the middle of an all-night 100 proof mass suicide mission, Earle waltzed away with a steamy August night and twirled himself into the middle of a wide, yawning field of summerfallow. Eyes closed and nicely pickled by the hootch scored that afternoon, Earle's gangly frame see-sawed and swung like a crane into the sopping heat. A stringed puppet, he danced, bobbing and lurching, his seaweed hair gone wild. A giant stomping the prairie sod flat against the horizon.

The sky yawned above him and for miles around nothing stood higher than a furrow. He stood aghast, a tiny pillar in the midst of the prairie. The stars rushed at him like diving swallows. Both minuscule and massive, Earle's body convulsed at the space around him. His knees gave way and, trembling, he flung himself to the ground, arms wide, blubbering. Like a beached merman he flopped there, screaming, "jezuzjezuzjezuzjezuzkr-jezuzkrjezuz." Spit fell from his mouth to the dusty ground, beaded, collected there, began a river.

The technical term is agoraphobia, a fear of open spaces, but there was no way the word would have come close to entering our monosyllabic minds.

Jojo, always the sober second thought, always the voice of reason, was the only one with the legs to go get him. But even he had overindulged in the dry raking wind of the godforsaken prairie. There is something about that amount of space that makes people think they can go slightly mad without breaking anything. He began the long winding journey out towards the sprawling giant. It seemed to take hours. We watched Jojo's route become more and more circuitous as he moved away from the tents. Straight lines curled around gravity's finger and sent Jojo tipping towards the four winds. Stars spun around the north pole of Jojo's nose. He trudged on, never seeming to get any closer. Like two forlorn constellations above, swinging to and fro, never touching.

Finally, by accident, Jojo stumbled up to Earle. Two ants on a stretch of dirt. Two mythic beasts on the Plains of Abraham. Jojo grunted and fell to one knee over the prone giant.

Earle turned to look up, his wet face transforming as wild panic gushed from his eyes. Above him, adorned with a crown of stars, the face of death loomed, threatening to crush him into oblivion. It grinned.

A fleshy fist levered out from Earle's side and knocked Jojo back on his ass. As if grappling with the reaper, Earle crawled to strike him again. And again. Finally both seemed to faint or fall asleep and it wasn't until morning that Jojo's cuts and bruises could be tended to and Earle could be rescued with a blindfold.

The field held no trace of their struggle except for a narrow coulee eroded from the flow of Earle's drool and Jojo's blood as the liquids made their way to the banks of the Missouri.

The Abject

Leeches. Buckets and clear jars filled with leeches. "Most versatile animal in the world outside the cockroach," the Professor would say draping a large fat one across the knuckle of his index finger.

He was also an expert on cockroaches. Explained at length how they were carried over from Asia by spice ships, how they were insanely prolific, how they were the very first flying animal in the history of the world, and how they would most surely over-run the country by 1920. He would catch one between two fingers and it would crackle and lurch to get away. These denizens of dark cupboards and feed-sacks held his attention for hours, a strange mixture of horror and fascination playing back and forth across his face. "Orthoptera," he would whisper as if to release some magic power. "Blattaria orthoptera, dulce quod utile."

But it was the leeches that held his attention most. Native, abundant, the lithe scavengers were his trademark. He was the one, the only Professor, the Leech Professor, the man who stood apart from the freaks and gave their histories, the genealogical circumstances of their births, and the medical analysis of their conditions. Professor Jules Offner kept the certificate of his degree deep in the side pocket of his medical bag.

When he first came to the show in '95, his very first examination was of a boy with a cataclysmic skin condition who came looking for work. The boy's entire body was covered with lesions, scabs, and shingles and the Professor probed him with the same revulsion and compulsion he did the leeches. The expression on the Professor's face pulsed as if he smelled something long dead, as if vapours emanated from the glistening skin, winced as if convinced something would leap free of the boiling sores. The sores were not from a recognizable disease but had clung tenaciously to the youngster from birth. The boy's eyes remained hooded throughout the exam. The Professor probed and took samples of pus. He asked the boy and his father questions about treatment, about the mother, about their ethnic background, their work. Plug stood to one side, hand on his fleshy chin, watching carefully.

The Professor stood up abruptly and, addressing Plug, pronounced that the boy would not be fit to perform. The audience would not be entertained, just disgusted. There is a difference. There was no angle or story to pique their interest. If the flesh resembled alligator skin or fish scales certainly—people loved notions of bestiality, of perverse unions. But a boy with oozing skin? No, it just wouldn't sell.

The boy went away with the same expression. The Professor washed his hands carefully in a white porcelain basin. Godliness, he thought to himself. Godliness.

Leeches were bigger farther north. From the small voracious ones he found in Kansas ditches, they gradually increased in bulk up to mammoth Canadian-size ones. These grand-daddies of the leech world took on personalities, the largest of them with striking green and grey shades along their backs. They moved by suckers at front and back like an inch worm or, in open water, through an entrancing, rippling motion, the flat of their bodies like rudders or wings.

The one he dangled from his index finger spasmed quickly and wrapped around the finger three times. The Professor gasped and scraped at it with the edge of a book. The book was a volume on skin conditions called *Epidermal Disfunctions and Their Causes* by E. J. Caruthers. The Professor was quoted on page 39. He had dreamt the leech would latch on and suck all the blood from his veins. It was a dream he often had; the suckers converging, the invasion, the dry incandescent shell of his body left to blow in the wind, crumble to sand. Such a tenuous defense.

His panic mounted and he staggered, water sloshed from the bucket. It tipped one way, then rocked back, falling over completely against the Professor's hip. The pages of the book were stained yellow with water. He slipped on one of the larger leeches, skidded on the water trying to right himself. Falling heavily, all he could think about was the clean, smooth surface of his skin. An integrity he cherished above all. But leeches twisted and convulsed all around him. Curled in a ball, he began to cry as if convinced of his own volume, his fragile container, the measure of his mortality. He cried long and hard, cried like he was cleansing himself of water, like he was expelling a poison through his eyes.

Tears streamed, dripped down. Salt stung. The leech fell free.

Undertow

Rebecca knew the Professor, knew him like the skin on the back of her hand.

Payton came swaggering in with him at his side and introduced Professor Offner to the sideshow. The balding Professor recognized Rebecca and carefully averted his eyes from her direct gaze. The history between the two spilled out into the tent like a challenge, like crossed swords. His credentials were a degree from the University of Boise and work in New York City fighting the influenza outbreaks. His eccentric bedside manner made him an unlikely candidate for family practice and the sideshow allowed him the opportunity to do his odd research in peace. But his history of unusual procedures was known to at least one of his co-workers.

Rebecca refused to acknowledge him under any circumstances. He did not exist to her after that first day.

The Professor was the voice and architect of the freak's stage life. He held a fistful of power in the show, so his presence procured an equal dose of deference and suspicion. After securing his position, Offner felt at ease enough to look on Rebecca with scorn. Her cold reception was not worth concern. The past was past. His power coated him like a preserving glaze. But when she walked by him, his eyes would often dart to follow, as if hoping to see a crack in the armor of her anger.

From the outset, his presence changed the aura of the freakshow. Deformity seemed glaring in Offner's gaze. "Spectacular," he would croon, "absolutely spectacular." Potential freaks would come in for an interview or get referred by other shows or dime museums. Plug and Offner would make the call; freak or not freak. Plug would mingle with the performers in his own repulsive way. Offner would not, refusing to have anything to do with any of the freaks. His relationship to them ended with his appraising look.

A rumbling growl began deep in Rebecca's throat. She told no one else what she knew about Offner. But she knew and he knew she knew. That was enough. For now.

Exposure

Cardinals were slip's favorite bird. Cardinals and whiskey jacks. And bald eagles but those could hardly be called just birds.

Annie was a bird-charmer when she wasn't being organized. Every stop she'd unpack her wood bird feeder and white porcelain bird bath and set them up near the edge of the backyard lot nearest trees. She'd stay until the first, usually a sparrow or chickadee, came and ate out of her hand and then she went back to her business. The kids joked about birds making nests in her beard.

On extra bright sunny days she'd take photographs of the birds with her camera. Once she took one with a cardinal perched on slip's shoulder. When the picture was developed though, slip was outraged at the drab depiction and would not accept the gift. The photograph was something slip could not accept, the suspension, the translation into glossy black and white.

The only other subject Annie regularly photographed was the audience. On the dime museum circuit she would part the curtain at the blow-off and snap a flash picture at the penultimate instant. When Chris was performing, this meant the moment before she threw off her cape to expose her one full breast. Annie told Chris about her photographs and she howled at the thought. Snidely she shrilled, "Ya, catch the bastards with their pants down." Chris' act seemed to have new spring in it after that, as if the thought of Annie and her camera gave her new impetus to perform. The audience would stand there, leaning, expectant, wide-eyed, unaware of the lens trained on them. Chris' smile meant so much more than they thought.

At the sideshow performances she would carefully wait until one of the other freaks held the audience before pulling the camera from beneath her seat. She liked this less because then the audience was not facing her, so the pictures didn't capture the full effect of their voracious gaze. Here, to remain inconspicuous, she did not use a flash and often the exposure time meant blurred motions and odd ghost images.

Once, on an especially dark night, Annie had slip sit perfectly still in the center of the sideshow crowd. She set the shutter-speed super slow. When the picture came out there was slip sitting prim and proper in the midst of wild arcs of movement, vague forms, and a host of ghost faces peering back out of the mist.

Her second summer with Sells-Floto she integrated the camera into Plug's pamphlets so that it claimed she was an amateur photographer. She would then pull out the camera as part of her onstage personality, gayly asking the audience to pose while she took pictures. This way she was able to snap shots of the audience looking right at the camera, where they would put on faces, poses, and look disconcerted by the lens' avarice.

She collected all these pictures in a scrapbook and we'd often sit in the dining car and page through it. We noticed the differences in the gawking faces, the wide variety of moods and atmospheres, the qualities of light, clothing, expressions, their complexions and emotions, the shapes of the gaping mouths, the distances between each member of the audience, the ways they leaned into the scene. We took pleasure in looking back at them this way, especially those pictures where they were unaware of the camera. The pictures that rested in our hands were like contraband. We would huddle over them protectively, feeling like we had done something wrong. But our nervous laughter loosened up with the quiet confidence of Annie there to support us.

We had them. They lay clutched in our hands. We passed them around, making jokes about the hairstyles or the goofy faces. We talked back to them, calling them names, telling them to go back home, get on with their miserable lives. Pencilled moustaches and glasses appeared on the pictures. Some were ripped up, tossed in the fire.

The King loved the scrapbook most, examining each picture over and over, nose almost touching the pages, looking for the secret. Riveted, he would stay up all night after we had wandered away. Searching for something. Or collecting something.

On the other hand, slip hated the book. While we peered over each other's shoulders to see the pictures, slip would sulk at another table and try to change the subject. Pictures held nothing, no recognition, no connection, for slip. Once in a while slip would hold one of the pictures against the real thing, a wagon or train car, but slip always chose just to look away. These pictures were story gone mad. Story gone ballistic. We saw memory in the pictures, slip saw nothing. The pictures submarined slip's tenuous hold on the floating debris of living. Slip had no room for certainty. No room for absolute.

Annie titled the scrapbook, "Misshapen: The Sells-Floto Sideshow, 1897–" and continued adding to it until the day she, and the book, disappeared.

Genesis (and then god came to earth, couldn't account for the freaks, went back)

Don't you see, people want to sleep forever.
But the audience was waking up.
We were asleep in their stories, they were asleep to dream us. All very tidy. Just call me the Ghost Lady and send me wandering the groaning hallways of your slumber. A floating light, a lesser light, formless and void, unstable as water. But send me knowing it is you and your insatiable eyes who are the exiled. You, standing outside the velvet rope, fitfully unaware, applauding like a dog jerking in its sleep, the rabbit just out of jaw-crunch. Our likenesses float near despite your best efforts to draw margins, create a scale, set a mark upon the dispossessed. Don't you see, that beautiful dream you've been taught dissolves in the presence of my skin. The question becomes. What is a monster? Or rather, what is monstrous? The façade crumbles in the wake of my breath, laced with bile and all the humiliation I've swallowed. Pressured by blood, by the sound of my words, it cracks, and startled, wakes.

For the audience, I wish insomnia. For the audience, I wish toothpicks to hold up their eyelids. The dry rush of my voice. I am not, will not, be satisfied. Cheer then. Cheer then. You bastards.

I will not turn into a pillar of salt, but soon, soon, I must rest.

Not (Xenia, Ohio)

Like a grasshopper on an eyeball. Like an ant on a scab. Spittle dripping down your chest. A cracked lip bleeding. A crushed cat on the gravel road and the crows stabbing at pieces. The sharp scent of sweat between your legs. Singing piss. A needle snag under nipple. Vomit in a disintegrating paper bag. Dust caked in the hollow at the base of your throat. Trigger finger stiff with cold and the horse's broken femur sticking through the skin.

A dandelion set on the bed in which I was hiding in.

And it wasn't even noon yet.

An Alibi

The second summer of slip's education included a few sidelines that nearly got out of hand. In any profession there comes a point when there is no turning back. The world buckles around the vocation like a cocoon, the worker firmly wrapped within. The work clothes come to mediate between you and not-you. And then there comes a point when the disavowal breaks down, disgust breaks the spell, and the act of betrayal, the betrayal of self, becomes clear. For slip, this point came when thieving slid into taking money for sex. This worked out fine until the night it meant killing a man.

Rebecca reaches across her body, leans out over the edge of the bed, teeters on the edge of the bed, and hits Rice hard across the face. Open handed but hard.

That's for killing a man. Damn, I never brought you up to live a shit-life like that. Damn you."

Rice sits stunned, jaw stinging, seeing stars and swirls, and waits to find out what the slap was for.

Men and women came calling at slip's door after the lights were shut down. Night after night, bills clutched in their hands drifted onto the bedside table. Two rules were clear; no penetration and no rough stuff. These rules became a mantra slip spoke at the door. For the most part it worked, but the crew made sure someone was next door in case of trouble. A pistol was behind the books stacked on a shelf above the bed.

They came to lie with slip. Some of them just to lie with slip. Some would press their thighs and belly into slip's thin back or bare hip, pressing and rubbing, breathing faster and faster until they stiffened, gasped and fell away. Some wanted slip to touch them, would close their eyes and lead the child's hand over their skin, through their hair. They would find the spot with slip's hand, that perfect sensitive spring of nerves, find it with a jolt and press the small fingers down, the smaller hand a warm buffer between their own hands and themselves. They stared into slip's eyes with their mouths open soundlessly, air rushing, rushing to burst red in their brains.

Latent Deeeeesire

And there was something inextricably erotic about the buzz and tumble of the circus—the frantic anticipation of preparation, the show like clockwork, seething and adrenalin filled, with its many tumultuous crescendoes, swooping motions and turns of emotion, and then, after, the lazy exhausted clean-up and wind-down.

Different cities, different air, different lovers but, at the same time, the assurance of sameness, the same hands repairing the torn bannerlines, the same performers sharing shoes and a last-minute shot of Keefer's gin, the sameness of squinting in the mirror every morning and not seeing the curves and blemishes that move through the world in a common direction.

And yet it was these same curves and blemishes, my thin hips, the laceration at the edge of my pubes, the exit hole under my arm that gets infected every spring, these possessions held close, it was these that I touched at night, a touch saying, yes, yes, bravo to all the plenitude of being, bravo to the Ghost Lady, the tent flap open with a flourish to the crowds, all the crowds there have ever been, a touch that lets them come charging awe-struck into my crotch, a touch which dispenses with audience, dispenses with display, turns riotous, arcane, gallops across the stage of my belly, shouts author, author, screeches indignation, finishes with a virtuoso flourish, a quivering finale, and shatters the spectacle, spreads, spreading, spreading the touch performing itself inward.

This is the way the world ends.

Encore, encore.

The Bowery (A Theory of America)

New York had turned bad for a lot of us: the crowds leaned too close, too frenzied and at the same time, at ease and confident. Each set of eyes, each gaping mouth seemed assured that it could kill or adore at whim. The Bowery cupped performers in its palm, invented the flourish, the contract for all future entertainment transactions. America had generated mass production, the automatic revolver, the telephone, the typewriter, the cash register, roll printing, an assembly line auto-mobile—but by far its greatest achievement was the audience which swallowed all these devices in one gulp, sucking every last taste of death.

It was at some point, on some perfect snowy evening in New York City, at the moment when the show began and expectation had reached its peak that the American audience and its spectacle were born. The lights went up, the actor assumed a pose, a sword raised above his mouth, and the audience began chanting, began to thirst for blood, began to beg for the perfect image. The ultimate commodity, floating in a fluid world of visceral shock and association, culminating in a flash of light and shadow, grew hands which reached out, arranged and directed us, created the camera, and finally, the motion picture.

New York became a city in shock, the ultimate city run riot at the asshole end of the nineteenth century.

This is the way the world ends.

Resistance

"There ain't nothing profound here Jojo. Nothing, hear me. Only profound here is that vacant look you get from the clown, a glimpse of shaking hands. Only profound here is the lies, the lies and the brute truth of staring faces. Only profound here is filthy dollars and cents. And none of that is profound in my book. Not a fucking bit."

Chris stands above and behind Jojo near the bannerline. Hot Texas air bowls from the south but the stars spike the canvas tight. Jojo is hunched in a furred parody of the Thinker staring at the treeline of the Mississippi a few miles over the corn. Chris was beat up a few nights ago. Clothes ripped and ribs cracked in a few places. Broken, Chris heard them taunt with harsh-edged words, pervert, freak, but whispered back, no, no, you've got it wrong, hermaphrodite. They threatened to crack her jaw wide on a rusted train-rail, placed her mouth wide against it, held a boot above, poised just above, poised—the dull clack of teeth against steel. The ligaments of the world threatening to bust open. She didn't scream, didn't scream, didn't scream, and they wandered off, dissatisfied.

Jojo is really weeping, not thinking.

After that Chris began changing her name. First every few weeks but then more often, announcing in the morning who she was for that day. Standing at the door of the dining car, she would introduce herself in a loud talker voice; "Aaand all the way from Paaaaris France, the one, the oooooonly . . ." Some names got repeated, mostly big names like Papa Bernadette, Fontina, Georgio, Solomon, Prince.

Sometimes, on less auspicious days, when she ducked into the dining car late, when her rouge was streaked and blotchy, her names were reduced to letters; Bee, U, Deedee, or Em.

Of course, slip loved the new names and meticulously called her by the proper name-of-the-day where others got it wrong, stuck with Chris, or avoided addressing her altogether.

Preservation (Peru, Indiana)

Salt. Everything tasted like salt. From the canvas, from the years of sweat, from the one tear I have left. Salt. The entire show made of salt. Salt to flavour, salt to preserve. Leaving salt in the air, in deposits on the grounds like a dried up sea. Long after the seagulls gulped the dropped soggy popcorn, there was salt.

Salt to preserve ourselves from ourselves. Salt to numb. Salt so a wound, any wound, would sting, sting like madness. So at the show, you could not have wounds, anything but open wounds. So they called them something else. Not wounds but something else. Anything but wounds.

Memory

Let me try to remember elephants for you slip. Let me try elephants.

First was the green breathing like underwater. Breathing close inside your ear the sound of names of grasses and vines they wheezed wet lily pads and hibiscus. First was the wishing like breezes in eucalyptus and orchids in loose lids of palm leaves flung open a flap of ear. First before sight could separate skin from wood, trunk from beam, ribs from walls. Before the glow of white painted letters Elephant/Kheda on the reinforced gate. The first *e* botched and barely discernable in the dark.

Second came eyeglints and a slow search of trunks like tree limbs. The hook. Or a bale of sweet alfalfa, a fist-full of sugar beet leaves, a bull-hand checking with a lantern, a ghost with empty hands. Straw shuffled, a wood-groaning lean and a trunk floated. Touched your neck. Eyelids. Nose and the cow exhaled sweet ferment like spirits diving into your throat. Giddy. Oat straw pricked your ankles. Two more leaned, the stall shifted around them. The oldest cow squinched her eyes, seemed to chuckle. Gave you a bump in the crotch with her wrinkled scabby trunk. You ducked through the gate and the walls were gone or breathing. Left rear hip against your shoulder, a flank behind, a tail twitching at your ear and a bulbous old head square in front. Sigh. Breath. Stomach rumble. Lip smack. Shift shift shift.

Lean shift sway and there were two calves in the corner. Smooth slick skin quick in contrast. In ordered concentration they spun and circled. In unison they rehearsed their act over and over. Just before you moved away to leave them be, one missed a cue, the other stumbled, turned, slapped her hard on the rump.

Shame, panic. They resumed.

A labyrinth of limbs bumped, squeezed slip out quiet. Breathe deeper. Swaying to the turn of the earth.

Echo and Decay

A FUUUUUUUUROR AT THE SHOWS, FAIRS, AND CELEBRATIONS IN EUROPE AAAAND AMERICA. UNEQUALLED IN ORIGINALITY AND UUUUUUUUUNSURPASSED IN NOVELTY. A POSITIVE SEEEEEEEENSATION. THE MOST AAAASTOUNDING AND AMAAAAAAAAAAZING EXHIBITION (softer) OF ODDITIES HUMAN EYES EVER BEHELD. FOR YOUR ENTERTAINMENT; THE CONGRESS OF HUMAN WONDERS. (With a flourish) LAAAAAAAAAAAADIES AND GENTLEMEN, STEP RIGHT UP.

The sideshow should have bored you to death but every day you got out there and flashed that infamous grin and you were, for all intents and purposes, a real cherub for three hours three times a day. The Singing Cherub slip. Love-blind wonder followed you everywhere. You were never nervous, waiting impatiently for Plug and Annie or Thsk to turn the crowd in. We stood waiting on those busy nights for the crowd. On the slower stops we didn't even need the caller, instead letting the crowd drift in on its own while we did the show continuously. It was hard not to yawn or let that blank look creep onto your face. Hard not to believe you were a machine.

We had our ways of helping the turn. Earle would mimic Plug's spiel word for word so there came from the tent a strange haunting echo. Jojo howled and barked while King laughed a screeching maniacal laugh. Anything to make them wonder. Anything to cause a stir, a rumour, a ripple in that unending crowd, anything to pull them into the galvanized space of the tent. Let there be floodlights! Let the adjectives begin!

And in the twelfth month, rest.

Gone Bad (Dryden, Ontario)

One set-up it rained and rained so long and so hard that the field next to the tracks turned into a lake. An entire arcade wagon sank beneath the mud and later we found out a feed man had been sleeping in it. We hoped he hadn't woken.

Slip kept repeating the nonsense words 'must egg' over and over with a glassy-eyed stare as the crews strained to move the wagons to higher ground. It wasn't until decades later that I realized that he was saying 'muskeg' and what that meant. A stray memory of his northern childhood and that landscape somehow lodged there where other things rushed by.

Later that night the flies came out in bushels. Flies and soggy gobs of dead or dying frogs. The mud was red and stuck to everything. Some of us thought it was the end of the world. Stuck to our rooms. Others wrapped themselves in tarps to get away from the flies. The locals whispered 'Wetigo' and left us to fend for ourselves. It wasn't often the circus felt like a stranger. But there, with the rain clinging to every inch of our sanity, there where the flies entered mouths, noses, ears, buzzing and biting, the weight of them wrestling you dizzy, there where the northern lights broke like a curse—there, the circus was not wanted. Not equipped. The coloured tents, the lamps and spangles, the face paint and drums, did us no good.

The lost feed man's name was Shag and he was fond of knock-knock jokes.

We lost three others that night, three without a trace, gone running into town or the woods or lost in the mud, sinking slowly with last thoughts piling up into the night sky. We would never know.

A dead frog was lodged inside the heel of my shoe.

We stayed in my room, slip and I, listening to the

screech of timber, the rumble of blood in our veins. We huddled together like an implosion, our fear seeping together. And we lived. Lived, even when skin deep was far too much.

Knock knock. Who's there?

Ah, just as I thought.

A Theory

It was Ms. Annie Jones who usually organized a day-trip into the town. She'd get us all dressed up proper and tell us a little about the place; its history, or what the townspeople did for a living, some dark secret, or just a landmark, anything to set it apart.

Each town came rolling over from the horizon like a crack in a wagon-wheel. Flint, Lima, Wausau, Ithaca. Over and over the plain gawking faces, all looking the same. They'd pretty much throw out their money the same frenzied way. We all dreamed of Berlin or Vienna or Venice, dreamed of performing in a stone hall with plush red curtains and uniformed ushers and gargoyles under the balcony seats. We were tired of small town America. But Annie, she'd dig into a town looking for its heart, some blemish like a new act she wanted to add to the show.

Annie was tall with long auburn hair. Without her bushy black beard she would have been one of those women the townspeople respected, unmarried but well-to-do with a business of her own, and all the men would watch her cross the main street with envy and faint fantasies of Annie riding up and sweeping them off their feet. She wore faded colours and comfortable Charlotte dresses she always seemed to be hiking up so she could walk faster and set things right.

We'd always go to town on the last day, the last show the night before and the crews still loading up into the afternoon. This is because Plug didn't want us showing ourselves and losing business. "Absolutely no freebies," he'd remind as the train pulled into a town.

Annie began by finding a nice restaurant. When we had all bundled in, side-stepping and trying to console the wide-eyed diners, we'd sit down and Annie would firmly lead us in prayer. I looked up and watched the others bow their heads, watched Annie as she spoke the words; "Give us this day our daily bread and forgive us our trespasses as we forgive those who trespass against us. Lead us not . . ." Always slip's head would bow deep upon the words "give us this day" and would repeat just those words over and over while the rest of us went on. Give us this day. The rest of us lost in our world of rights and wrongs, property and exclusion, temptation. But slip stretched the s's out; "give ussss thisssssss day, give usssssssssssssss thisssssssssssssssss day."

Annie'd watch slip too, glancing up quickly from her prayer. I could see her mind working at why slip seemed so desperate, the urgent s's making her wince. Our eyes met over slip's plea. We wished we could answer prayers. Theories began to pass between us like a gravy boat, but I knew theories alone weren't going to make a miracle.

Canada Watches

The show made several forays into Canada while you were with us. Always, in the back of my head, I feared losing you. Feared they would see through your disguise and take you away. Looking back, I realize that I was also fearing they would see through my disguise. I felt like an imposter, posing as a mother. The Canadian crowds looked straight through me.

Those crowds in Windsor, London, St. Catharines in Sherbrooke, Cornwall, Kingston, in those alien-seeming places like Sault Ste. Marie, Thunder Bay, and Winnipeg, all watched the show in a distinctive way. Nothing obvious, but Canadian crowds had a different feel to them. They leaned back instead of forward. They were very quiet, didn't rustle and whisper like most. They sat like an open book, waiting to be entertained. I felt exposed. They weren't doing their part. They weren't inventing the glamour. Sometimes their attitude seemed like snobbishness. Most times though, it came across as nervousness, as insecurity.

I remember a young girl came up after one show in Brantford. She was tiny, thin and pretty and even smaller for being so shy. She sidled up to me and asked in a stutter if she could have my 'oughtgraph'. "I guess I oughta," I chirped and crouched down beside her. When she talked I could hear slip's voice in her intonations. There and not there at the same time. Language in her mouth became a denial. A negation. I was lost in her mouth. Lost, but not afraid.

I was lost in all their mouths. They waited. Waited for us, on stage, to tell them who they were. Most crowds shouted us into existence. In Canada, we were expected to be the creators. We re-crossed the border with vertigo. Vertigo thinking about the open O of Canada's mouth.

Recognizing Revolution

One glaring hot day, Annie, Jojo, and I ended up in the dining car sipping on some fresh iced tea with Wilder. Wilder squeezed an extra shot of lemon juice into each of our glasses with a wink.

Annie turned to me and looked me square in the eyes. I remember this because not many people looked the Ghost Lady square in the eyes. When someone did it was a remarkable event. Annie did that day and she said, "Rebecca, are you happy with your life?"

I was stunned. More by the fact than she used my real name than anything. Was I happy? Good lord, how was I to answer that? The sweetly sour tea washed over my tongue as I stalled for time. They were looking at me too intently.

Jojo leaned across the table toward me as if he knew what was coming. I felt set up. I stammered. I fidgeted. I blurted, "I get by, that's enough, considering." I was already guessing what they were up to. Word was going around that "rights" had to be upheld. That we all had "rights." Freaks had "rights."

At the time I remember being a little worried that I was going to lose my job. Worried that Jojo and Annie, who both had the confidence and language to think about these things were going to get me kicked out of the show. A surge of anger washed though my gut and I said evenly, "Be careful what you do, my friends. There are more things at stake than you think. You may be a woman who looks like a man and a man who looks like an animal but I am a black woman whose mama was a slave. Don't tell me this living I've scraped out of nothing isn't mine. Don't tell me my 'rights' are going to leave me on the street back where I started. Don't tell me anything unless you are speaking for yourself."

Rattled, they sat back and the silence sifted away the speeches they had ready. Annie stared at me, looking as if maybe she hadn't seen me before. She heard me. I could see she was turning things over and over in her mind, trying to find a middle ground. I gave her credit, decided to come half way. "Are you happy with your life?"

She smiled. Her whiskers bristled around her dimples. She moved her chair closer and said, "Well, let me tell you what would make me happier . . ."

Later that evening, long after Jojo had ambled off to bed, long after all the iced tea and ginger snaps were gone, we found a middle ground. I would help her when the time came, provided that she discussed these things with everyone in the show. Everyone. I told her that her confidence left people out. She thought about that but I don't think she quite understood.

As we walked back to the sleeping cars she asked how slip was. I was hoping she'd ask. I told her about slip's lack of memory and how I was coping. She turned to me in the dark, shocked. "That's incredible. You mean you actually tell slip stories to fill in for memory? It's ingenious! What stories do you choose? You must be exhausted."

Finally, I had someone to confide in. We sat cross-legged on my bunk until morning just talking about what a strange creature slip was and how much love it took to fill in all those missing moments. We fell asleep there, curled into each other, thinking about slip, about how slip had to reconstruct a past at the same time that the freakshow had to forget its past.

Syntax

A change came over the show's workers in the summer of 1900. While the show went about its business and we all did the grind and the gruntwork and the poses, something had changed. There was a sense that we were part of a larger pattern. If not a larger pattern, then a larger significance than the daily drudge and oblique satisfaction that the circus life doled out. Something more.

As if convinced of this, the hands named the train cars and the wagons like they were war horses or ships: Liberty, The Etruscan, Restraint, Apocalypse, Merganser, That Fine Divine Intervention and Magic-Making Machine, Quixote, Suffragette, The River Ganges, Duende, Boer. Strange long nights of thought went into the naming as if the hands were convinced the names would be carried far and wide: The Orient Express, Three Fates, Phantasm, Genesis, Galileo, Gawain, Workers Unite, Frankenstein, Napoleon's Toe, The Pheonix, Leda, Overture, La Esperanza, Vertigo. Come off-loading time the shouts above animal grunts and squeals were dizzying and beautiful. Poems rumbled through the near-dark. Histories arranged themselves, new mythologies were created, political spectrums dissolved. And they went to sleep thinking that the next audience, that audience tomorrow, that audience better hold on to their hats.

Props

Drenched wet, Rebecca and slip scuttled under the awning of a newspaper stand on the corner of Bowery and Rivington near the end of Third Avenue. Beer gardens ran as far as they could see down Stanton. Men lounged under tarps and umbrellas, secure in the gut of the Bowery. The woman with kid in tow continued down the street, looking through the rain for 229 Bowery and a green door leading to the third floor.

Sadly named Lew Blackmar, a man at Epstein's in Chicago had given Rebecca the address, telling her that her photographs would be an "indispensable tool in her career aspirations." The man was a toad but he knew the freakshow business. She had put it off for a long time but on this trip to New York she decided she'd better if she was going to keep her profile among the winter dime museums. She knew slip would hate the ordeal of a photography session but when she left the grounds the gravity pull between them kicked in and they found themselves hip to hip again. The train down from Albany was blissfully tranquil but now the buzz and stomp of the city made them both jumpy. The rain fell harder.

Two hundred twenty–three, 225, 227, . . . 231? They backed up and saw a narrow doorway tucked back in a dank alcove nearly blocked with empty fruit crates. The 229 was painted green like the door and the frame and the wall around the door, even some of the windows. The two flights of stairs smelled like stale bread.

The photographer's name was Charles Eisenmann and he had made his reputation taking pictures of freaks and carnival curios. The Freak Photographer. He was tall and lanky with a handlebar moustache and balding head. He wore a suit-coat and grey vest with a striking light pink bowtie. The smell of malty bourbon wafted around him and he held a cut crystal glass as he ushered in the bedraggled figures.

Eisenmann abruptly exchanged a few pleasantries but, not offering a drink, he got down to business. While he set up his equipment, Rebecca inserted her needles, and put on a stark black toga. A grandfather clock clicked its tongue in the corner. He motioned Rebecca onto the set and placed her against a metal back support stand that ran up to the base of her skull. A stand to help her stay still. Facing the camera, the shutters whirred, she stayed still.

Still.

The backdrop was green with splashes of red. Vague roses emerged from the blur of watercolour.

Longer yet.

Still.

The lights tickled a trickle of sweat between her breasts. Her ankle itched. Still. (Hold the face, hold the face!)

Stayed.

Still.

And then Eisenmann emerged from behind the camera, assuring her it had been a good one.

While he unstrapped Rebecca, slip burst from a fit of boredom and snuck behind the camera. It smelled like raw alcohol and smoke. After shuffling a metal case under the machine, slip stood on tip-toes to look into the lens. There, Eisenmann and Rebecca were untangling. They both looked up at the same time, Eisenmann still with the buckles in his hand, Rebecca uncomfortable, lines of strain inking out from her eyes. They both stopped, looked at the camera as if expecting it to flash. But slip just continued to watch. They stayed still. Waiting.

Eisenmann's head pushed at the top of the picture frame, setting the composition off-balance.

Apocalypse

And there the camera stood. Eisenmann encapsulated behind, like a slick puppeteer. Rebecca posed, steel cold against her spine, part of the apparatus, part of the tableau. It seemed to be a scene set for a third eye, looming, perhaps laughing at their odd postures. Eisenmann stooped over, hunched like an ancient man. His eye pressed desperately against the eyepiece. He lifted his arm above the thick black cloth cover to point which way Rebecca should lean. Most of the time his hand was flat, meaning stay still. Rebecca stood bewitched, staring hard at the lens, wanting to wave, make herself into the perfect image of herself, greet herself through the lens with a perfect immortal smile. At the edges of her discomfort and intrigue was fear. Fear that the camera would breathe the light straight through her, that she would be blown apart by that black maelstrom, that imploding iris. The violent repercussions, the aftershocks of an instant in time threatened to fuse her to the watercolour screen propped behind her. Vaguely, unknowingly, she feared this. Like a faint imprint on stone memory she feared this. Reached to touch her lips, blew Eisenmann a farewell kiss.

Light/Not Light

On the way back from Eisenmann's studio, slip stopped in front of a store window. The rain had stopped and the clouds had broken so that the sun was out between the large cumulus towers. The blue sky seemed bluer by contrast. In the reflection of the window, slip was cut in half by the sun, half lit, half in shadow. The store was a fine bookstore and seven leather bound volumes were propped up and surrounded by red velvet linen in the window display. Slip stood so that the reflection in the window fell onto the cover of one of the books. The sunlight reflected off slip and lit the storefront slightly, as if slip were a lantern, a lantern held by a half stranger, a lantern held up to itself, squinting.

R

I fell in love with an albino dislocationist named Rob Roy. Yup, the Ghost Lady and Rob Roy, we were an item. Off and on for several years we'd meet while wintering up here in Baraboo. The last winter before it ended we even saved up enough to take time off and jump the train down to Sarasota. Spent two weeks on the beach hiding from the sun. A burn would have killed us. He was sweet and gentle. Worked the east coast circuit in a tired, resigned way. I think it was because he hated his body—hated the way his joints popped out and he could unhinge himself. He could slip his knee joint and bend it back like a bird—no one else I'd ever seen could do that one. Crazy wrists. His bones clicked and snapped so loud in bed we had complaints from King next door. He could embrace me behind his back better than any man face to face.

He began to bring me flowers, began to lead me by the hand on the riverbanks, began to insist I take care of this ramshackle body. He'd come to my room with pears and rhubarb and asparagus, left them on my step when he thought he might be getting too intrusive.

We were married on the Fort Gibson Ferry at Muskogee. The ferryman looked like a pirate with a patch over his right eye and the right side of his face paralyzed. We fed him vows and odd poetic musings to repeat and he dutiful pronounced us man and wife. Seagulls yelled from the prow. As a wedding present, Rob caught a monarch butterfly and passed it carefully into my cupped palm. Its wings stuttered and then pulsed, its legs tickling my life line.

When we landed on the west bank, Rob told me his real name. Robert Vancourt. And so . . . Rebecca Vancourt. I looked up surprised. He was matter-of-fact about it and I thought offhand, well what's another name. No big deal. Rebecca Vancourt. I repeated my new name back to him. He grinned. "No, Vancouuuurrrr." Vancooor. No, Vancourt. Vancore. No, roll your *r* like this. Rrrrrrrr. No

Nononono. I couldn't believe he was being such a dink. Vancourt. I couldn't say my own name right. The gulls got irritating.

Things were never the same after that. Polite but no thanks.

He died of a hemorrhage late one night when the crescent moon dangled limp from the sky. And once again I felt like a lonely freak.

And all these years all I can think of is what Rob and me could have been. Rob and me, albinoes in love, the ultimate white wedding.

EXPATRIATION

No one realized it was him.

The bally turned well for such a cool night. Toledo had been a tough stop; not much money and not much gaiety. Smokestacks lunged against a patient sky. On that night the crowd knew more than we did. The tent buzzed and necks craned toward the middle of the floor where a knot of men stood in a tableau of nonchalance. Not until the blow-off did it drift up to us that President McKinley was in the audience. Then it was obvious, and from the stage we saw him smiling, stroking his dark moustache and shaking the odd hand. Backstage we sneered and watched as Chris nervously walked onstage. From where Jojo and slip crouched next to the drums they could see the President. He was plump and red-faced but as Chris began to undress he became entranced. Chris could see it too.

She was gonna do it. We knew it.

In the middle of the drum-roll finale, Chris stopped, held up her long thin arms. She said in her most feminine voice, "Hey, Prez, wouldya like a kiss?" Chris stood in sheer black briefs and a cape. Her one breast had glitter around the nipple. The President consulted his aide. He pondered, not daring to look at Chris. Finally, to the crowd's delight, he began making his way to the stage. Men cleared a way and then helped hoist him on stage. The stage was higher for the blow-off and the President ended up kneeling at the edge of the stage, Chris standing above him, extending a gloved hand to help him up.

Dusting himself off, McKinley turned to the crowd and said, "They told me office would be tough." The crowd chuckled but they were nervous. The president standing next to a half-and-half? What was the world coming to?

"Well, I guess no President can claim to have done this before," he said, still loudly, but now turned toward Chris. More chuckles.

"Are you so sure?" Chris answered, eyes hooded, sultry.

McKinley continued to smile at the crowd and move in to kiss with exaggerated motions, his left hand on Chris' shoulder just above her breast. Many men cursed themselves for not having a camera. The President pulled away and Jojo saw lipstick on Chris' cheek near her mouth.

There are all sorts of inaugurations, I suppose.

The President waved, made the victory sign as the crowd cheered wildly. This was much more than their money's worth. They all knew the papers would never take the story—who would believe it? And besides McKinley controlled the press pretty well. Ever since the railworkers bowed to his demands and the Dallas *Star* had been shut down, the press stayed clear of McKinley. His statements to the press were clear and precise, tailored for easy processing, and there was nothing more to say.

He stood for a long time on stage, his face glowing with relief and excitement. All at once he felt that he could do anything, America could do anything, the world was theirs to have. Standing on stage with Chris Christina, McKinley sensed the audience, felt their eyes like never before. They thought he was invincible, and so he was. Standing on stage with Chris Christina, the President learned how a crowd can create immortality.

Camouflage

McKinley, despite Chris' kisses, declared war on Spain after the *Maine* was sunk in the West Indies. The papers grabbed the reins and rode off to war and the whole country had no choice but to get swept along. Eyes that were normally glued to the sideshow now were more interested in the papers and the pictures that came back. Spain became the freak.

The aerialists from South America and Jorge, the iron jaw from Mexico, spoke Spanish and feared for their safety. Late at night the hands gave them English and Italian lessons to hide their accent. Until dawn they struggled to soften their vowels and flatten their intonations. Their tongues went numb under the strain.

Hispanics crowded at the gates looking for refuge. After the show Plug was beseiged with pleas for asylum, desperate attempts to impress him with mediocre juggling or feats of strength. Some were let in but many more turned away. A critical mass for the show was reached quickly. Desperate faces pleaded for a job. The performers bullied Plug into hiring a few more but it was never enough.

Luckily, we had experience sheltering persecuted people. Three years before, a group of Navaho travelling through Nebraska approached Annie in Davenport. They were half-starved and fleeing the army who had slaughtered thirty members of their tribe in a valley near Hastings. We altered their skin colour with some ointments I stole from Offner's cabin; harsh oily stains that I warned would not fade for months. We gave them inconspicuous jobs scattered through the show, jobs that multiplied easily. I told them they would have a chance to learn what it was like to be a ghost. But they already seemed to know that. The tall young chief who spoke to Annie was named Screaming Eagle. During the week and a half he was with us, he gave Jago knife throwing lessons and tended to three ailing horses in the menagerie. Once close to the Canadian border they slipped off before dawn. They gave Annie and me an eagle feather each in gratitude. Canada seemed a long way away at the time.

The week after we had taken on all the Spanish-speaking refugees, Payton came in and cleared house. But by then the show had cleared the city and the worst danger from the keen-eyed city police was left behind. Jorge and the aerialists passed as non-Hispanic, Payton fooled by their make-up and their careful words. Payton wore an American flag pin and mentioned the "war effort" three times as he squinted up at Jorge's eyes.

Surface Tension

The other freaks made jokes about my affairs. The Ghost Lady's Ten-in-One Love, they crowed. I let them talk. The gossip was harmless, just chiding jealousy.

The best I ever had was Os the glassblower. He got on in Akron and the next show he blew a blue glass kiss that stilled the shuffling crowd where they stood. I watched him work from stageside, watching his tongue and lips, wanting to meet him inside that shimmering glass. I loved the way his lungs sounded.

I asked him to blow me a jug for fresh milk so I could watch the cream separate and pour it off. He asked no price and mouthed the words "milk" and "cream" as he pumped the bellows awake. I watched, sweat trickling into my palms. He raised the glass to his lips with the mouth hoop and as he blew our eyes met. He smiled and the container went lopsided, following the contour of his smile. When he did not mind, I knew I would let him come to my bed that night.

Holding a glass of wine he said, "Good Lady, I am sorry to say that this suitor you have prepared is sadly impotent," and my shoulders drooped, "but . . . he would be honoured to assist in any other task you might have." His eyes pursed into my lap and his lips glittered.

There, the backs of my knees in his palms, he invented my belly all over again. Invented the space inside, invented the lip, the trembling spout, invented with breath and kiss and slow. I thought I would harden and congeal around his tongue but every night, his hands like bellows, he told a new story, mouthing the words as we moved close.

I kept the milk jar in the shape of the breath from a smile and I was afraid I had become transparent.

Theories

One show the crowd tried to rip Jojo's hair off. They thought it was fake, wanted to see the embarrassed man underneath. They ripped and tore at his coat until it bled. They would not believe the hair was real. Either that or they wanted to make it fake by the force of their numbers. Jojo escaped only when the hands and the rest of us threw ourselves into the fray. Jojo stayed in his room for the next three days, talking to no one except slip when slip would carry in a plate of stew or chops with pinto beans or hash and he'd just start talking low and steady like someone had been there the whole time.

"My body goes deep, and high, and long sentences it rolls out a scroll of prophesies for me to pore over, decipher the lines of fingerpad, eyelids, iris. Canine incisor. Measures there are many, standing against my length, width, circumference. Shades, divisions, types I read like a topography, marking my place over next to the landmark of your gaze. (Space to lose one's way? Become disoriented? Disappear? Missing Persons Anonymous, Inc.) Ours and yours. Datum to be arranged, evaluated, implemented. A trapeze trajectory. A writer with a juggler's ambition. And I wonder at my desire to be knowable. At the categories of their horror, the zones of paranoia traced like defended borders, passing customs with trepidation for the last time. A sixth finger grows from my wrist like a fetus beneath the skin. Divination of spectrolosis, the scientific charts turned jazz and the control specimen lost in a crowd (ah, the crowd, the new tyrant of our lives) of infinite variables. Hypertrichosis, elephantitis, microcephaly; it just depends on who the talker is, doesn't it? I sometimes dream that they succeed in tearing off my hair and in the dream I am not bleeding and sore, not at all, in the dream I am normal when they are done. And then there are other times I dream of normal hands running through my coat. And sometimes that touch is the most violent thing."

Violences

A theory of tickling. Fingers on the bottom of the foot, against the belly, back of the knee, in the armpit. The tender searching nerves on the arch of the foot, the fleshy stomach, organs flinching under pressure, joints, tendons exposed, open to a quick motion, paralysis. A light touch, feathery, yet insistent, like a tick about to plunge its head in to suck, bloat.

A theory of vulnerability. Squirm and laugh but panic is what you want. There is trust here, and terror, a strong desire to escape. Anger or fear is not allowed, instead laugh, laugh it off, beg, beg with tears streaming, beg it to stop.

A theory of power. A giggle becomes intoxicating. Access to another body, these private places, the tickler tickled by this privilege, presses further, drunk on trespass. This other body spasms with pleasure (the tears they are of joy, of course, they must be out of joy), this other body trapped under quick fingers. Quick fingers already near. Laugh it off, laugh off this feeling of invincibility and satiation. Play it again, the tickled other crumpled at your feet.

A theory of violation.

Barely

Taking refuge in Rebecca's bed, slip's face glowed, giddy with pleasure, a large yellow bruise taking form, covering the once pink cheek. The child-thief had just killed a man. The night air, razored and poised, had flung past slip's headlong retreat across the grounds. Pure experience rushing, veins full of the double-sided surge of adrenalin. Jago came saying he had heard the shot. He sat by the bed listening to slip's story. After the shaking stopped, slip's hands stared back in awe, words laid claim and stilled the blood.

The trick had turned bad. The mantra's spell had been broken. Rules are made to be supplemented.

The man wanted to be slip's father. Said, "I want to play your father," as he stepped up into the wagon. A father, sharp as a blow but slip acquiesced, eyes hooded. Your father. What would playing father involve? It was a question.

First it involved servitude. An infernally long night stretched out. The play was about control; standing above, a vulnerable neck, a precarious straddling, moving unpredictably, making the space his own, all with gentle motions, shy smiles. He was a large angular man, hair just graying, crackling blue eyes with a square blocky jaw. The type of face that led council meetings with candid humour and grace. His orders this night were quiet, but edged with slurs, growing thicker. Brandy dribbled onto his bare chest. Taking slip's hand in his, he asked slip to come away with him. Be mine, he pleaded fervently.

An answer stuttered on slip's tongue. A father. Be mine. He reached to pull the small body closer but slip twisted away. No.

Stung, he asked, "Why, why when you can live normal, grow up normal, loved."

No, not ever. And slip pushed the man's hand away again.

This continued until slip asked the man to leave. He glared, his raised voice seething, "Are you a freak too? What are you hiding?" But slip pointed to the door. And the man cracked, control blasting into rage.

The room blurred; flying linen, overturned table, a broken mirror. His large body seemed to fill the room, steal the air. Scrambling against the bookcase, the gun tumbled into slip's hand, warm wood stock and bolt leapt under tiny fingers just like Jago had taught. The man laughed at the quivering barrel. Approached. A slow motion hand raised, descending, and then smack. Struck. Falling backward, slam! The gun flew from slip's hand, back and behind against the wall. Luke knelt, part of his neck missing. He stared, eyes levelled. Shifting slightly, slip reached, picked up the gun, pulled the bolt back again. Luke stared. Slam! Red spread in a fan like brandy down his chest. The hole looked absurd and too small. Like an angry pimple. Nothing really. He toppled backward, landing with a crunch on broken china.

His body did not seem out of place in the room's disarray. The gun still held tight, slip dressed and stood over Luke. The bolt snapped into place again. Slam! His neck collapsed completely, wet air rushed out, his head lolling to the side.

The payment for the evening had drifted down next to his head from the dresser. With a grin, slip crumpled the bills and stooped to tuck them into his mouth. Tidy.

After listening to the story, Jago and Rebecca tucked slip into sleep. They hurried out together to wake a couple of the hands and persuaded them to deal with the body. Four of them hoisted Luke into a large gunny sack and hauled him off to the river. His horse was sent galloping back into town. The red-stained linen thrown in a stubble fire—the sharp scent of the fire unchanged. The blood on the floors washed easily out the door and down into the dirt. The gun, lifted from slip's sleep, was buried deep. Tidy.

From then on, every morning, Rebecca would tell slip in private, "You killed a man, you killed a man, you killed a man and smiled, you shot a man and he will never again wake to the sun like you just did, blood spilled on your hands." Endlessly, she reminded him. Gone was the adrenalin, the high, the flashing lights, instead, Rebecca's stern face. "You shot him three times. He will never know the smell of fresh straw like you are now. You killed a man, slip. You killed. A workmanlike piece of murder. Murder. If there ever was a mission, this will be mine. His name was Luke. We hid the evidence but you shot him three times. We sunk his body deep but it had three holes. He's crappie food now, but he once breathed and laughed. Three times. Killed. Luke was his name. Luke. The police might forget but by god you never will. Ever. This will be mine."

And Rebecca looked old.

"How it is you found me come to rest here in Baraboo I'll never know. From the looks of all those posters and pamphlets you got tucked in your folders, you been following names and talking a blue streak for a while. Tough job that. Not much to go on I'd imagine. Them names don't mean much in the show—change them at the drop of a misbegotten dime. Like ghosts."

"Ya, ghosts, except in ink and paint and on people's lips as they look at their feet trying to remember and me begging. Begging. Becca it's been hard. People don't understand what I need like you do, they resent my questions and think I'm stupid and they leave things out and they . . . they think I know myself."

"I know you, Rice."

"You know me, Becca."

"Let's stop talking for a while."

Ink

The beginning of the end came with the words; "Whereas the press and public . . ." There was no turning back. The silence had been spoken, the contract broken. I was aghast. I had told her I would support her, but I was still terrified.

I knew Annie had been working on something of this sort for a long time. A manifesto, she called it. She'd ask questions, got people drunk safe in her wagon so they'd tell their most painful, most secret, most desperate stories. She'd have that look when Plug or someone crossed her—a look that said, "Just you wait, just you wait, I'm working on it."

WHEREAS the press and public of both hemispheres, without just cause, have for many years past gratuitously and voluntarily bestowed the term freak upon all human beings differing in any way from ordinary mortals, and

It was inevitable. A machine grinds and grinds and eventually comes to a halt, the mysterious inner parts tired and worn, a screeching protest heralding the end.

Annie whipped us into a near frenzy. We lounged in the dining car as she read off our new constitution. She came in and began reading. In a commanding voice she sounded exactly how I imagined freedom. Or was it too melodic?

Feet that had been propped up fell to the floor. Hands went to chins in consideration. Forks stopped shovelling. Nods.

It was Sunday, June 15th, 1899. No turning back.

WHEREAS the term freak is approbious, without any scientific meaning in an anatomical sense, and
WHEREAS we feel that the term so unjustly conferred upon us, with or without our consent, is an indignity, and

We had trouble listening. It was difficult to follow exactly what the point was. The word "Whereas" threw us off. The sage Wilder had used in the supper stew wafted in and some of us smacked our lips, hungry again. Annie growled, she talked of higher ideals, of action, of a united front. She banged the table with the flat of her hand;

> WHEREAS, because, fortunately or otherwise, we are possessed of more or less limbs, more or less hair, more or less physical and mental attributes than other people, and might be taken as additional charms of persons or aids to movement, as the case may be, and

Faces twitched, fingers drummed, brows furrowed. What was this woman telling us? What . . . why would she . . . ?

I became acutely aware of that bearded woman standing in front of us. Her body was shaking with fury. The small space became full of her. Oh, how could I have such thoughts at a time like this! At one point she looked at me, stared straight at me, and the two of us held that connection for several minutes. "Charms," she said and looked down briefly from my eyes, as if thinking what I was thinking. The Ghost Lady and the Bearded Lady revolved around that small room, the idea of emancipation like a stunt waiting to be invented. The idea of freedom subterranean and lusty.

And then, a few more nods, a few eyes turned up to her fervent face. I, too, nodded, and it was like I had thrown myself into her arms. Memories flooded back. She was speaking us back into ourselves;

> WHEREAS because we, differing so from the ordinary or regulation human being, in that we have certain marked and distinctive characteristics of mind and body, we hold that difference to be no reason whatever for being called freaks . . . therefore, therefore, be it

Therefore it was. Resolutions, safety nets against trespasses. "Therefore," Annie's voice boomed resoundingly across our bodies. "Therefore!" we left saying, "Whereas!" we shouted to the flat face of the show. Therefore there was no turning. The wheel left its axle. The machine groaned.

We marched to Plug's tent with copies. Tossed them on his desk as he stared at us, dumbfounded. Poor Plug. He didn't even know how to read. He just sat there, stunned and immobile. I suggested we find Payton. He was staying at the Royal Jefferson and he, at least, would understand the full ramifications of this manifesto.

We marched down Washington Avenue past the state capital with a breeze coming off Lake Mendota. People watched us, but there was such purpose in our step they dared not gape too long. We hardly noticed them. Annie and Jojo led the way, their hair ruffled by the wind.

I followed, wishing only to run my fingers through their whiskers.

INHIBITION

There was fear too. I know because I felt it. When you are shaken outside yourself into someone else, even if it is someone else dearer than the un-person you were before, there's still that lurch, that gap of vertigo, that in-between when you can't turn back as history slides into the next era. And you have no choice.

And yet it felt like a long time coming. Deep down I knew the crowd that stood comparing themselves to us, to us, the dog-face, the albino, the pinhead, the midget, the giant, the half-and-half, the bearded lady, the man with wings, the fat lady, ruthlessly fitting us into neat worlds of horror or fascination, tidy categories of excess, romantic notions of good and evil. It could never last. And a bearded lady would come and we all faced judgement day with our bodies hot and fidgeting in the chilly air.

This was to be a reckoning. We stood outside the Royal Jefferson shouting until Payton emerged stern and huffing. We were not going to engage him in a war of threats, we would surely lose that.

He came out on to the stone steps. The Royal Jefferson boasted a Victorian-style architecture with fake spires and stone facades. It would have made a great theatre. Instead it lodged the wealthy and famous, hosted business luncheons and conferences, headquarters for business and royalty in the midwest. He did not look alarmed. He took the papers politely and with a mumbled promise, "I'll look at it." And then he turned and disappeared into the hotel.

Emanicipation was a word that dissolved as soon as it was spoken.

That was all. "I will look at it." That wouldn't do.

Jojo gazed up at the impenetrable building and raised his sing-song voice against it, "Prepare! your toils only begin; for we soon shall enter upon a journey." The challenge crackled with intensity—not hatred, but pure passionate certainty.

Later that night, the Royal Jefferson burned. No one was hurt, the fire was started in the unused back wing, but it spread slow and sure and consumed the whole building. The stone arches blasted into shards from the heat. By the morning there was nothing left. Nothing. Even the ashes blew away in the brisk northern wind that swept from the lakes.

Another Theory

Jojo and Annie tried desperately to make sense of the world. Jojo, with his Great Dane thinking frown, would piece through the events of the freak show, the uncanny circumstances that brought us all together, the violations that threatened to rip us apart. Annie would stomp and fret, a large bird in our earth-bound existence, a giant bird turning metallic and hard, making the crowds wince with her velocity.

Some of that thinking and energy rubbed off on the rest of us. Hard to imagine a Ghost Lady like me theorizing anything but in my own way, I began to think about the show, the place I had in it, who watched and who posed, and where the money flowed. These things I noticed.

And through it all, through the grit and the ideals, slip flitted like a butterfly in a machine.

It is late now, the sky out the wide window has turned a burnished orange and a deep glow caroms into the room from the horizon out of sight to the left. Noise from the interstate drifts in.

Rebecca and Rice fall silent, exhausted, but dogged, determined to go on. Rebecca is searching for the next anecdote, the next strand of story, Rice compiling all the information, trying to make order from these hours of talk, hours of information. Both realizing that there would be no satisfactory end. No end at all.

As if on cue, Ricky pops his head in to tell Rebecca her other visitor had arrived. She perks up and fusses, "Well, come on then, let's have him in!"

Ricky stands aside and the door remains open, empty for the longest time. A dry rustling noise drifts in, a slight movement at the edge of the door frame, a brown beef-jerky hand grips the wood, and then a face. A face like a freeze dried plum sweet and leaking eyes. He moves inch by inch, shuffling around the corner, static snapping around his knot of white hair. His pants ride up almost to his adam's apple and his back is so hunched it reaches higher than his head. His neck and pelvis seem to have vanished. Clutched in one hand is his violin and bow. Not until he is almost at the bedside does King Sirrah look up. His eyes swirl, focus on Rice, and clear for a moment. He grins a great gum-drooling grin, grins a great glomming geek sort of grin.

With long breaths in between each syllable, "Little shit," he says, "no bother, ma wallet be empty as a."

Rebecca laughs and beams up at him.

He turns toward her and shuffles in close to lift and fluff a lingering kiss on the back of her hand. Wrinkles fold in, meshed. King's eyes sparkle, "Pleasure, as always, will."

"Well, slip's got me doing it again, King. I'm trying to remember all those old show days. And slip wants it all! What do you think of that? The nerve."

King holds up a finger, sets his violin to his chin, draws the bow across sending a long trembling note into the room. It *ends with a scrape and a soft resonating echo. Rebecca nods. Then he beckons to Rice with a finger, motioning nearer. Rice comes to him. King leans to whisper, wheezing in between words,* "Well, we fooled 'em for a long . . . time." *His breath smells like the sage Rebecca said Wilder put in his stews. Rice knows that was a very odd sentence for King to say. It was complete. Rice looks over to Rebecca for confirmation. She nods. (So this was memory, Rice realizes.)*

King straightens, looks out the window, clear-eyed, "Fooled 'em good." *He teases a few small mischievous sounds from the violin, looks at Rice.*

"But tell us about yo' own self."

Resonance (Wheeling, Wisconsin)

Goddam 6:30 a.m. and the King dragged us all down a goddam gravelled road east of town, talking the whole way. "And justice will be." The sun crawled along the horizon and we were crabby, not appreciating King's humour. The air was wet, water glistened on the bent leaves of dandelion and fireweed, and a mist rainbowed over the road. We passed copses of alder and pine, following blindly as King leapt and gestured on ahead. "When there is no, then just."

With the sun in our eyes we had no idea where we were going but suddenly the rolling hills cracked into ridges of granite. The road swung right but King took us down a trail to the left through some insanely green saplings. Outcrops of stone loomed up on either side and we found ourselves in a gully facing a large cliff-face 20 yards across a steep incline. Veins of quartz criss-crossed the mottled granite and a few scraggly pine trees clung to its face. The sun had just reached the top of the trees and the line between shadow and bright moved visibly as we stood there. King pranced with his arms outstretched as if he had invented the whole scene.

Wilder unpacked and passed around some biscuits. At that moment several of us realized that he was our mother.

King stepped down below us on the slope and began playing his violin. Not his usual scratchy noise but slow smooth notes that glided up to the cliff and came diving back again. And then again, the notes swelling and accumulating in the intimate space of the gully. Huge spirals of sound spun upward threatening to lift us. And then again, thundering through our lungs and throats, piling against our tongues. And so we sang. We sang at ourselves, high terrifying notes and low guttural bursts that told us we were alive. The stone, our hearts, like a drum.

The sunlight careened down the stone face, the notes like ushers. And the sun settled on our backs, the music on our chests. Pinned there, we fell into relief against the rock. Huge shadow figures slid and blended against the rock. Distorted giant ghosts we could barely connect to ourselves.

A hand raised to say hello. Hello. And the brilliant gullet of earth received us.

I believe King was trying to tell us we were there.
I believe we were.

REVULSION

The newspaper crackled in the door, anger pushed, snapping, threatening an invisible paper cut where it flew:

12c. **The *New York Times*** Tuesday, August 4

* * * * * * * * * * * *

──FREAKS REVOLT!!──
INDIGNANT HUMAN CURIOS MAKE DEMANDS

"Fuck!! Look what he's doing! He's turning it into a publicity stunt. And he's changed all my provisions. The bastard!!! I should have seen it coming, should a known it was too good to be true." Annie collapsed into an unstable wooden chair with the paper crumpled in her lap.

No one knew what to say.

Angus Payton had twisted Annie's words, taken all her nights at the typewriter, and turned them into a farce. Worse, turned them into an embarrassing portrayal of freaks, full of arrogance and angst. Worse, turned those words into a profitable hoax. Worse, printed the farce for America to gawk at and use for their amusement.

The muckrakers loved the story and all of William Hearst's papers ran it front page. I think it was the first time the word "rights" had been used in print to apply to a few individuals rather than the American public as a whole. In the sensational aftermath, that small victory was forgotten but Annie tucked it away as a minor victory in the midst of overwhelming defeat.

Annie imagined Payton and Hearst sitting in their overstuffed mahogany offices, hunched over her speech with red pens, chuckling to themselves. The image made her ill. She spat and the chair creaked beneath her.

The show was about to head back west after lolling in upstate New York, drawing on the City during the holiday season. Tourists splashed in the new Ashokan Reservoir in the Catskills, doing family things, throwing baseballs and building castles in the sand. The sideshow stuck close together, standing at a distance and watching the daylight dwindle. Everything was unreal; the water, the colours of the beach umbrellas, the laughter, the great sand-castles that legions of children made and destroyed and made again.

As night approached and the show wound into action, the sideshow huddled around Annie in the dining car, stunned by Payton's treachery. The news had done the freaks in. Now, instead of freaks, the performers were "prodigies." Payton's version painted our demands as extravagant claims of superiority, as requests for the public to recognize us as more than human.

More than human.

We were caught in his machine as surely as beasts of burden.

Annie's disgust ran back and forth between resignation and rage. We didn't know which emotion won out when she left the car. She walked out and my heart broke. Not a clean break, but a twisted wreckage, twisted as surely as Payton had twisted Annie's hypnotic words. Twisted beyond recognition, useless and embarrassed, my heart not my own.

Annie disappeared after the show that night. I'd like to believe she bolted, took off and made good somewhere else. But there was a rumour on the rails that she showed up at Payton's winter home in Newcastle, tried to set his garage on fire, and was hustled away by some of Payton's men before the police got there. A Penn-West boiler man swore his nephew saw her led away from the blaze by the elbows.

In Kingston and Ploughkeepsie the crowds had the news folded in their coat pockets, threw tomatoes and stones at us. "Proooodigies!" they shouted in derision. Not until we reached Olean a week later did the tension cool. We missed Annie and there was not much life in our stage poses. Even though we'd been turned inside-out, turned against ourselves, even though the same old same old had us caught in its clutches, something, something had snapped. The spell was broken. The show became just a show. The flash of a hand of cards to collect the winnings. Our lives ballooned as we suddenly saw the world outside the confines of the backyard.

The Great Lakes met us at Erie, let us submerge ourselves in the quiet slate grey of a cloudy afternoon.

Chaos

Unconnected from. The point being.

At 4:38 a.m. wearing only underwear and a rich green Havanna cigar in the pitch black, Angus Payton climbed the ladder to the highwire. No one was around. He was from a long line of circus men and he climbed the ladder with a showman's flair even though he had never climbed one before. He has watched often enough, studied the bravado, the arm flourishes, the sure-footed ascent to heaven. He was not asleep but felt weightless nonetheless.

This was not nostalgia, Angus was not looking wistfully at the stands. He could not see a thing. By touch he climbed and climbed the swaying ladder. The crisp air nipped his plush skin. It was not sleepwalking but might as well have been.

Angus was brought up to stand at a distance, look out over a landscape, brought up to assess, not by wonder but by surveillance, arrangement, management. An empire hinged on this gaze. His father Angus (Gus to those who knew him well) and his grandfather Angus had the same eyes. In some ways this last Angus had failed his predecessors. Here he was managing a second-rate circus, a circus of which he didn't even own a majority. While Carl Sells and Montgomery Floto provided all the financial backing and sat comfortably in their New England cottages, Angus was slaving away, calling in zoning connections and dealing with the petty squabbles of 120 employees. Hardly a traditional Payton way to live.

The show threatened to engulf him. He could deny its passion no more.

On the highwire platform he turned away from the dimly gleaming wire to face the invisible stands.

A few days before, a tiny waif came up to him and asked him, out of the blue, "Do it again." He had seen the child flitting through the business of the grounds but never paid any attention. The big-eyed face looked squarely into him and his blustery composure receded behind a nervous chew on his cigar and a quick look around for an escape. But the child had him. He had to speak to it. (Was it a little boy or a little girl?) "What can I do for you, little one?"

"Do it again. You're the big aga aren't you?"

Aga? What did that mean? "Yes, yes I am. But do what again sweetie?" A wink, that always thrilled the little tykes.

"Nothing." And Angus had never seen such a sad face. "Will you hug me?"

Oh god. Hug? He moved to tickle slip in the belly but got a curt "nuh-uh," the child's arms open wide. Good lord, he hoped someone was watching. A perfunctory hug.

The child squirmed into his arms and then tugged free, ambled off. Suddenly he wondered how on earth this child survived with the show. How on earth. Such a tenuous defenseless bit of life. The show-grounds were suddenly louder. The breeze whipped through the thick wool of his Cardell jacket. It was a lurch of realization that told him, in no uncertain terms, that he understood nothing. Nothing.

He reached for his watch to see what time it was, collected himself.

Angus crouched carefully, his legs unused to the heft and strain, the metal of the highwire platform digging into his bare feet. Poised there, he whispered an epitaph to the centerpole. To the centerpole he said softly, "Welcome to the greatest show on earth, welcome." He leapt into the blackness, arms spread wide, leapt confident, sure of the safety net of insanity, the welcoming arms of annihilation. He was sure it was his finest hour.

In the morning the bull-hands found him impaled on the metal chairs nearest the rings. The seats entered his body so completely they had to use crowbars to remove the chair legs from his wreckage.

Combustion

One afternoon in Chicago, the one showhand who could read ran into the dining car with a *Tribune*. He pointed to a serial the paper was running on the American sideshow. Jojo read it to the rest of the troop and as he read we realized that this writer was different. This column knew the sideshow. The freelance writer was Allen Jones and when Jojo finished reading he looked up and said, "You know who this is, don't you?"

Then it clicked and Annie Jones was alive again.

She was somewhere around Chicago writing freelance under a pseudonym. Her writing was subtle, not too confrontational, but enough to raise eyebrows and counter traditional views on the freakshow. She attacked local politicians in a playful way with a sharp sardonic tone.

We begged and stole to get the *Tribune* wherever we were, disappointed when her column wasn't printed. It was like she'd never left. Only now she was made up of ink on newsprint, verbs and exclamation marks.

Princes and Prophets

Ninety-nine was a tough one and we ended up wintering in Kohl & Middleton's Palace Museum in Minneapolis. Dime museums were closing down left and right. There was only one left in Chicago and that had gone over to a more theatrical program. The Palace stood as a crumbling bastion, and most of the clientele seemed to be older men and women leading sceptical youngsters by the hand. It seemed like a last refuge, a last stand; the thinning crowd became preoccupied with other amusements like the World Series and vaudeville. The performers were a collection of old veterans; the Ghost Lady, Jojo, slip, King Sirrah, and the renowned Prince Randian joined up as fall crumbled and blew onto street corners. These performers, a few pickled punks, an orang outang, and they had a world-class dime museum show going. A memorable swan song.

Prince Randian, know as the Caterpillar Man, rivalled King Sirrah as the most travelled freak on tour. He seemed old as the show itself. With an undulating convulsion of his bread-loaf shaped body and a deft roll he dropped off chairs and made his way deftly around the building. He smoked Durhams, rolling them himself with quick motions of his tongue. The rest of the performers followed him with their eyes and he was used to it, stopping before scooting through the door, shooting them a wink.

Prince Randian was the impossible. A wizened old head and a tight gunny sack filled with life, he seemed to defy the world.

"Wunna need those gangly limbs anyway," he'd say, "all de world should be beautiful as a bullet, just like me. No excess, no waste." His voice was low and gravelly, turning wheezy when he was winded, or hushed when he talked to just one person, his mouth close to their ear. He was a question without an answer.

Randian spoke with nostalgia about his youth in Bridgetown and his early performing days in New Orleans, talked with a commanding voice, a voice still threaded with the vestiges of a West Indies pidgin. His physical presence added to the story-telling, there was so little else to him; a mouth, a voice, those keen eyes waiting for a response.

A large impressive woman named Kana joined the troupe at his side. Manager, body-guard, wife, Kana spoke mostly French, so Randian had to translate for us. When he did she watched him closely, keenly aware that he could be changing her words on her. She had been around the show long enough to know the bare fact that who is speaking dictates the power. He seemed to translate faithfully, only changing the words with obvious delight and a sidelong glance. She would see his subterfuge and respond with a whack on the top of his head. "Ma princess," he called her when he was in trouble. Randian rolled and shuffled with surprising speed, the roll to move sideways, and a motion like an inchworm to move forward.

Outside the museum, Kana spent most of her time watching for dogs. Randian despised dogs, feared and loathed them. He imitated their lolling tongues and blank stares with relish and contempt. "Fugging curs and bitches, mongrels allaya!" And of course they loved him. They came trotting for blocks around to investigate this undulating form lurching down the sidewalk. Kana deftly wielded a stick and bellowed ground-shaking curses to put them off the trail.

While Randian translated, Kana told the story of how Randian was born with no arms or legs. Kana's back was straight so that her lungs could fill and she bellowed the story as if demanding the gods hear as well. She told us that on the day Randian was born, 48 men were hanged.

On that day the monkey-faced god looked down and threw coconuts at Randian's mother, named Fig by her master. Coconuts rained down on her and she threw up her hands and ran for shelter. But the monkey-faced god got caught up in his game and went too far. Fig had used up all the arms and legs of the baby inside her just to get away from the rain of coconuts. The monkey-faced god was embarrassed and saw that Fig was howling mad at him. Some good had to come of the situation. So, the monkey-faced god stole Fig's bile, stole it and filled the mouths of the 48 hanged men with her venom. It was a great amount of anger. More than even the monkey-faced god imagined. The men, all near death, suddenly writhed and bucked, their arms became ten times stronger and they were able to pull themselves up the rope, hook their legs around the branch and save their necks. The anger in their eyes sent the onlookers fleeing and these 48 men scattered into the bush, noose burns still raw on their necks. It was these 48 men who banded together, organized the resistance, and began the Courroux Revolution. The following year, the docks at Bridgeport were taken and the French sailed back to Europe in defeat. And that is how Prince Randian was born, already a hero of the revolution. And that, my friends, is why each one of us, all of us freaks, are heroes of the revolution. The end.

Kana and Prince Randian fell silent in the same instant.

Emancipation

Randian added a sense of peace to the troupe, a sense of relaxed confidence, a sense of completion that had never been a part of the show. Kohl and Middleton were hands-off owners so Jojo managed the show. He spiced up the performances, taking chances by allowing the performers to improvise and experiment. The audience lost its aggression. The velvet rope was stored away and the acts roamed freely through the audience. We found ourselves blatantly watching the audience, analyzing them, making conjectures on their upbringing and status.

The audiences sensed it too. They left the show dissatisfied, confused. They complained about being cheated. Gone were the gawks and prods from a press of bodies. Instead the scattered customers took furtive glances, kept their distance, left bored and regretful.

In the echoing halls of the museum, we became masters of the arena. We demanded propriety when the audience was unruly. We demanded attention on our own terms, performing more elaborately and interacting with the audience. Their eyes dipped and dove away from ours, they shuffled nervously through the room, they raised their blustery voices to fill space and comment on some minor item, pretending not to notice the living exhibits breathing so near.

The gaze had been turned around. Magic was a foreign word in this country by then.

Visibility, or Irony (or, how to be a lady)

One off-day Randian mentioned talking with Annie Jones recently, not realizing we had all worked with her in Sells-Floto. When we descended upon him for more information he made us promise the utmost secrecy, saying that her career depended upon our discretion.

"Well, you musta figured by now that she's writin' under otherer names, no? You suspected this much. But many many uh them, all sorts a writin'—and all of them with names startin' with A. J. Lots a them. And wots more, she's writin' novels! Novels! Ya, you all didn't know that now. Lots a them, all sorts—romance and adventure and politics just like the men, and not just wid A. J. She lets people figger out that trick with the A. J. and then does the real workin' on these great novels. You gotta be in love with this woman, no. She makes the odd show with dark dark glasses and not for long. Dressing up in the nice suits and spats. Anything can be fake, she told me. The rest be writin' like crazy, she a madwoman with the pen that Annie. You gotta love her. And the thing is, nobody knows which are Annie's novels except her. No one."

Looking

I was the one looked at. I was the one. And the looks they were rage.

Oh, I don't know, maybe not rage. Felt like rage. Hurt, right here at the base of my throat, stung like rage was being done to me. Rage beaming out like pan lamplight, panning past me, fixing me, piercing me there, pinned to a backdrop of mere survival. A dying, grasping at hair, blubbering, screeching kind of rage. Blind rage.

And temptation clung sticky and warm to the palms of my hands, clung to them as I cut through a side of beef with a dull saw in the cookhouse, clung to them as I spread rat poison and bread beneath the beds, clung to them as they snipped hair close to the root, clung to them when fingernails craved the slick gelatin of eyes. But the temptation left as soon as it came; another town on the road to the solace of winter hibernation. Temptation left, dripping from my palms, staining the things I wished to touch. Temptation left, leaving me a ghost, a thin gray wisp of pity for the gawking crowds, their potato bodies lost in midst of their cavernous eyes.

I'm not a vain woman. I'm not a spiteful woman.

I'm not a woman any longer.

I claim this title of Ghost, claim it with a fist, snap it off their tongues with my teeth, and swallow it whole. The Ghost Lady gone ghost looks back, looks at the crowd, looks out with eyes held high to the cresting waves of audience, looks straight past the loosetrigger gazes and sees the blood in their groins, the lumps in their throats, the sucking clasp of their lips, the panic in their shaking infant bodies.

Now they look through me. I flit against their eyelids like a moth in the dark, land lightly, wings breathing, and burrow.

Now I'm a pressure against the back of their eyes. A dark scuttle where they can't quite see. I wrap myself in silence, cocooned until wet new wings unfold from their irises.

Origins

One is the only one and shape depends—maybe becoming a few—on this order, with hands slick with clay, hands slick. Voices slip or ice into one last regret. Regret, the only thing preventing me from forgetting, forgetting my skin, forgetting a little bit that this story is told in a plain room.

Oh, I'm getting too cryptic for you slip. How can you translate your life into poetry when you don't even have the bare facts yet? How can I make your life magic when you don't even have a stage to re-enact it on yet? I am despairing, I can't do what you ask. There is too much to one life to shave it down to an afternoon of talk. I am not sure magic needs a stage. And does poetry need facts? I suspect you know all this, slip. And I am going to be one of those absent facts a few days from now. Let's talk about magic slip. Let's talk about now.

Forever

Animated age and the eyes of an old woman, Din the Orang Outang silently prayed for the planet. Silent with a great mouth and wide smacking lips tasting apocalypse in the air, apocalypse under thick nails, apocalypse filling her wrinkled dugs. Plant juice and seeds, suns and space. She abdicated her opposable stare, kissed, licked our eyelids as we slept, dreaming of a beginning, dreaming of thick fur matting our arms and bellies. That was no place for a prophet. That was no place for a goddess. So she howled once, late, late at night, howled that jesus wasn't an only child, howled to challenge the inevitable, howled to beckon madness to descend from the trees. She sat waiting, watching, with a piece of banana between her toes, watching your teeth grow long and keen.

An Exception (to) Theory

Don't. And even if it were a single mouth speaking it wouldn't change a thing. Voices aren't that easy. Things get lost. Wait for the voice—not for confirmation but amazement. Disorder. Fiction, as if convinced, goes on spieling. But the audience can't hold that position, can't maintain that pose. Blue grass and willows bent, bent, broken by the carts in the parade. What is worth? Am I easily digestible? Who is pulling and who is riding? The talker checks his pocket watch given to him the day after he was hired by his now ex-wife. Consequential. Other theories and theorized others. There is a small Canadian child looking for an old mulatto woman to tell him where he has come from. There is a Canadian novelist poring over route books looking for evidence, looking for that one magic night when the tyranny began, looking for a spiel to get him out of this predicament.

And the parts are held together tenuously, as if barely remembered. There is a question of authenticity. It may be okay that the audience is not quite convinced. The story can fall apart in places. That is okay. The story was murderous.

The Professor's diction was perfectly consistent. Perfectly. The freakshow stage never ceased to be approached.

Don't.

"But I know what it is you're asking, slip. I know and I have no answer. I can't keep telling you who you are. I haven't the breath for it. You gonna have to do some of the telling."

"What makes your skin white, Becca?"

A pause. "Oh, I see. King told you. Yes, I was born sweet chocolate brown. But that wasn't good enough. I dreamed of being white. Only Professor Jules Offner had the technology to help me. A thick white paste to steal all the pigments in my skin. 'Beautiful' he said to me, 'spectacular.' At the time I thought, go ahead, say it, go ahead, 'nigger'—he might as well have said it. He took my black, but there was still my beautiful black nose, my lips, my sweet voice, all that jazz I still had. White skin wasn't near enough I learned. But it was my own self that was to blame. And it did give me a living after all."

"Is there a paste to steal the white from skin, a paste to turn me black?"

The Ghost Lady lay still for a while, the question there before her. "Not exactly, but . . . " and she whispers something in Rice's ear. Rice nods, yes. Out from under the question, she leans carefully over the side of the bed, carefully, like she might break in two, and pulls a green tackle box from beneath. She props it open and looks up, "You sure this is what you want?" Rice nods again. She begins opening tubes and vials and mixing with an old bent spoon. Satisfied, she beckons Rice closer, holds up a paint brush with a black paste on it. "Weed-juice from the Professor." Rice leans in, face inches from the brush. "You know it's forever," she says and she pauses, waiting to see comprehension.

They stay like that for a long while—the brush poised in Rebecca's hand, Rice leaning over the bed toward her. Leaning, eyes not meeting. A quiet stroll around the word for a while. Forever. Leaning.

Rice whispers, "Yes, I know. I've always known that." Leans further.

"And all those stories you were telling me Becca . . .," a slick black paste begins to spread against Rice's white white skin, ". . . do it again."

∞
1997
∞

The Absolute Fake is the offspring of the unhappy awareness of a present without depth.
—Umberto Eco

POSTSCRIPT: PRESENCE

I had travelled down from Winnipeg to do research at the circus archives in Baraboo, Wisconsin. With a mixture of indignation and fascination, I watched as the history of the "freakshow" spilled off pages. Spilled through my thin fingers. I was looking for the exotic in myself but it was not there.

The books fell shut, the pictures stared back, handwriting refused me. Academics, books about race and oppression, essays on politics fell to the floor next to my hotel bed. Useless. Another language when languages are failing.

Falling asleep, my last thought was: I am going to have to relearn what search, what quest means.

Baraboo lived and breathed the circus. Old men tottered around the grounds, comforted by the din of the talkers, soothed by the blast of the calliope. They'd stop and tilt their heads as if listening to the spiel again, as if convinced everything was as it used to be. It wasn't. The crowds poured around them like they were statues.

At the archives, I pored over and over stained pages, sifting through the route books, autobiographies, diaries, posters, and old albums of photographs, looking to find the real "freakshow." Stacks and stacks waited there, waited for some misbegotten fool to dig them up. But I felt like a thief—the books filled with trinkets, the covers forfeiting their cool contents before my stealthy retreat. Staring out the dusty windows, the afternoons paraded by without recognition.

Recognition would have to come some other way. Recognition would have to come some other way.

It was only when I looked down, looked hard at the back of my hand, turned it outward at an odd angle, that a slight jostle of knowledge fell into my possession.

An old black man with a wild look in his eyes and a black-eyed susan in his lapel started to watch me from across the table. He had a pink scar across his chin that looked like a second set of thin lips. Without preamble, he leaned forward and addressed me, "Hey, pssst, hey slick, what you looking at?" The voice was accusing, suspicious. I pleaded ignorance, waved my hand over the open books. My nervousness seemed to assure him. His stare was unrelenting.

In a hushed run-on voice he told me he hated the freakshow. He thought it sullied the greatness of the real circus; the artists and athletes of the big top. With disdain he directed me to the hostel down along Hwy. 12 (next to the new McDonalds) where he said, "over a hundred years of the godforsaken freakshow was on its last legs."

I did not understand.

"You will see," and he got up and left, his pants sagging off his bum. He turned at the door, "You will see there is nothing to see, buddy."

I wasn't sure I had heard him right.

Left on the table where he had been sitting was a copy of Shelley's *Frankenstein* with a pencil stuck in page 39, the part where they pick Dr. Frankenstein off the ice-flow. A smell like vinegar, like old pickles, wafted around the empty chair. I was enthralled, rattled. Uncomposed.

Later, after I learned to read the signs, I guessed he was a retired clown. The wild look in his eyes and the quiet voice were the tip-off.

Are the most crucial stories always grudgingly told?

As if convinced this old clown would lead me to the secrets of the show, as if convinced this would be the last stop, I drove down to the hostel.

Uncontainability

There is no invitation. The hostel is quiet and musty. Dirty matresses lay in the hall. Syringes. No one seems to be there.

When I open the last door, Rice lies curled into a ball turned toward the window. It is 1997, the middle of summer, and Rice's tongue is crumbling into dust. A beginning or an ending.

I stay at the door. My eyes have nothing to land on, so they move aimlessly around the blinding bright room, the insubstantial figure on the bed, the illegible writing scrawled on every surface of that body, colours and script blending until they become indistinguishable. Names and places tattooed over and over, one on top of the other. Colours bleeding into others, every colour in the rainbow and many that even the rainbow wouldn't allow. There is barely space for me. I do not belong here and the sound of my voice seems far away, as if underwater. There is something monstrous about my presence.

I begin to ask questions desperately, as if the information will slip away as quickly as I gather it. I blurt them out and they barely make sense. They are not so much questions as denials. Still, I lean to hear a reply, affirmation, anything at all. I lean and learn to despise this position, hungry, ravenous even. My eyes, my voice eager to drink Rice up. Shame and desperation collide and disperse.

But I lean toward silence. Toward veils and gaffs and sleight of hand. Toward Rice's carelessly draped hand with its black tattoo sunk to the bone; your name is rice, the last word erased by layers of scar tissue. Scar tissue upon scar tissue until the original skin ceases to exist. I lean toward skin the colour of language purged, blind-spot black, green, green and deeper green, a dangerous violet, and red, reds veined with misdirection, splitting under this gaze.

ROBERT BUDDE

Robert Budde was born in Minneapolis, Minnesota and has lived in Alberta, Ontario, and the Northwest Territories. He is the co-founder and editor of Staccato Chapbook Press and has been published in *Prairie Fire, a/muse me, Border Crossings, can(N)on*. His first published book is a work of poetry entitled *CatchasCatch*. *Misshapen* began as a creative dissertation at the University of Calgary. It was primarily researched in Baraboo, Wisconsin at the Circus World Museum. Robert Budde currently resides in Winnipeg where he teaches English at the University of Winnipeg.